Thoreau's Laundry

Thoreau's Laundry

❁

Stories by
ANN HARLEMAN

SOUTHERN METHODIST
UNIVERSITY PRESS
Dallas

This collection of stories is a work of fiction. Names, characters, places, and incidents are either the product of the author's imagination or are used fictitiously.

Requests for permission to reproduce material from this work should be sent to:
  Rights and Permissions
  Southern Methodist University Press
  PO Box 750415
  Dallas, Texas 75275-0415

Cover image: Photo of the author's daughter in Moscow

Jacket and text design by Tom Dawson

Epigraph from "Questions of Travel" in *The Complete Poems, 1927–1979* by Elizabeth Bishop. Copyright © 1979, 1983 by Alice Helen Methfessel. Reprinted by permission of Farrar, Straus and Giroux, LLC.

Library of Congress Cataloging-in-Publication Data

Harleman, Ann, 1945-
    Thoreau's laundry : stories / by Ann Harleman.—1st ed.
        p. cm.
    ISBN 978-0-87074-513-3 (alk. paper)
    I. Title.

PS3558.A624246T47 2007
813'.54—dc22

                                                              2007002561

Printed in the United States of America on acid-free paper

10   9   8   7   6   5   4   3   2   1

For Brendan
For Tim

Acknowledgments ❀

I WOULD LIKE TO THANK THE FOLLOWING PEOPLE: DON BERGER, Joanne Brownstein, Rand Cooper, the late Sam Driver, Barbara Feldman, Laurie Fidrych, Bruce Flinn, Laura Furman (fairy godmother), John Harbison, the late John Hawkes, Brendan Hobson, David Hobson, Sarah Hobson, Timothy Hobson, the late Ilona Karmel, Alan Kimball, Margot Livesey, Sally Mack, Susan Mates, Bill Rice, Angel Rocha, Bruce Rosenberg, Lois Rosenthal, Cynthia Shearer, Ottie Thomas Smith, Meredith Steinbach, Gordon Weaver, Janet Hagan Yanos, the residents and staff of Tockwotton Home, and — with great affection — the members of the deep-hearted Providence Area Writers Group (PAW).

Most of all I thank Kathryn Lang, Gail Hochman, and the Girl Group: Gail Donovan, Elizabeth Searle, Frances Lefkowitz.

I am grateful to the Huntington Library, the Rhode Island State Arts Council, the Rockefeller Foundation, the Bogliasco Foundation, the American Academy in Berlin, the American Academy in Rome, the Macdowell Colony, and the Rona Jaffe Foundation for their generous support.

These stories, in somewhat different form, have appeared elsewhere: "Meanwhile" in the *Southwest Review* and *O. Henry Prize Stories 2003*; "Stalin Dreaming" in *Glimmer Train*; "Sharks" in the *Boston Review*; "The Angel of Entropy" in *Shenandoah*; "The Ones without Visas" in *Witness*; "Street of Swans" in the *Southwest Review*; "Iggy Ugly" in *The Virginia Quarterly Review*; "Biscuit Baby" in *Ms.* Magazine; "Thoreau's Laundry" in the *Alaska Quarterly Review*; "Romantic Fever" in *Primavera*; "Autumn, 1911" (as "My Romance") in the *Southwest Review*; "Will Build to Suit" in *Shenandoah*.

Should we have stayed at home
and thought of here?
—ELIZABETH BISHOP

Contents ❁

Meanwhile ❀

AT THE HOSPITAL I TAKE MY HUSBAND — HE WAS DEMOTED YESTERDAY from forearm crutches to a walker, and so hates himself slightly more — to the solarium. We proceed down the second-floor corridor, with its smells of pine and urine, at a bridal pace. From time to time Daniel casts an envious glance at my feet, though at this speed — the speed of the rest of his life, and that's if he is lucky — they might as well be bound.

The room at the end of the corridor lives up to its name, full of golden afternoon light. Amazing for December, the last notes of a long, molten autumn, the warmest on record in Rhode Island and (but they keep no records for this) the most beautiful. Poor Daniel has spent it all in this place.

The blind woman is here again. You'd think one terrible affliction would preclude others, but no: she's in this place — a rehab hospital — to recover from bypass surgery. Her husband — sprightly, cheery, always here — is feeding her lunch. *I don't have to do that, yet.* They sit by the long windows, sunlight striping the woman's face, seeming to fill her obediently open mouth. How beautiful she is with her cropped silver hair, her saint's cheekbones, her pale eyes whose blankness gives the effect not of vacancy but of looking inward.

She smiles in our direction—our conjugal shuffle has alerted her—though not so brightly as her husband. Mel—is that his name? I don't know hers, or rather, I've forgotten it, or maybe I don't want to know it. I think of her as Lucy, after the saint whose eyes were gouged out by the Romans. Or did she do it herself? Or was that Agatha?

Daniel and I play cards here every afternoon—simple kids' games, Rat-a-Tat Cat or Go Fish. That way, we don't have to talk unless we have something to say. He runs a hand over his graying, patriarchal beard, the way he used to when he was working out some complicated sociobiological concept. He gets mad when he loses. One more loss. *Should I let you win, darling?* But we haven't quite come to that. The room is full of sound: the Cassandra mutterings of pigeons on the long window ledge, nurses' hazy voices over the intercom, Christmas carols on a far-off piano. In one corner of the room is a fountain, new since yesterday. Water splashes joyously over red plastic dolphins into a red plastic basin.

What color is it? Lucy asks Mel between mouthfuls.

What color is what? Here, take a sip. Small sip! It's hot.

The fountain.

Blue.

I remember blue.

Her tone is only slightly wistful.

Prognosis. A word that always makes me think of "snout."

Chronic progressive multiple sclerosis (CPMS). Chronic = always. Progressive = worse and worse. Multiple = many (all up and down the spinal cord, which Daniel used to call the body's sine qua non: the marrow of the spine). Sclerosis = hardening (as in, hearts).

Date: November 28, 1999

From: graywolf@hotmail.com

To: lioness@earthlink.net

Subject: communicado

are you the first person on e mail ive ever wanted
to hear from   you   love

I spring Daniel for the afternoon so that I can take him to see his urol-
ogist. Doctor Jacques: wide, pale, gleamy-eyed, with a tilting, lyrical
accent *que j'adore*. It makes the most unpalatable truths sound hopeful.
His son has multiple sclerosis (MS), too. When his son's wife divorced
him, he was immediately courted by, and very soon remarried to, a
nurse at the rehab hospital.

Zis girl—Doctor Jacques says, taking off his flesh-colored glasses
for a smile that makes me feel twenty years younger—zis girl, she ees
so close to *le bon Dieu* zat she was still at sirty-sree a virgin.

Urine *urine* URINE.

Once, in the summer—it was hot, maybe August?—I got into
the car an hour or so after Daniel brought it home. He was still driving then, still going to his office at the university, where he spent
mornings shuffling slides he used to teach from and rereading his
own book, the one that won the Lamarck Prize, *Animal Dispersion
in Relation to Species Behavior*. I drove to the gym. Felt increasingly
damp, thought it was the heat. On the StairMaster, my bodysuit and
tights felt wet in the seat. Thought it was sweat. Then the odor began
to rise.

Why didn't you tell me? I yelled when I got home. Just fucking *tell* me? I could've put down plastic over the seat.

He was sad all evening because I'd lost my temper. He sat in the recliner with his eyes closed, his large head caressing the high cushioned back. Stress, he mentioned, makes MS symptoms worse.

Date: December 1, 1999
From: graywolf@hotmail.com
To: lioness@earthlink.net
Subject: yesterday

dear gorgeous lover
but first a message for the creeps & voyeurs
that im told have access to this e mail since it is
unerasable and about as private as sky writing if
this is the only artifact that survives me into the
millennium then yes, this beautiful woman and
ihave fucked each other and yes, we enjoyed it
enjoy being far too weak a word for the ecstatic
abandoned glorious inventions which delighted
us and will ihope continue to delight us in spite
of the inevitability that you creeps & voyeurs and
probably my dean will read our messages but only
to marvel at the endless capacity of our bodies
to surprise and transport each other now back to
the message which is i cherish you your precious
flowerlike pussy which istudied so devotedly and all
the rest of you

We missed you! Mel cries.

He is walking Lucy down the second-floor corridor, not (say) holding her elbow or linking arms with her, but towing her by the end of a red-and-green plaid scarf tied around her waist. Last week he lied to her about the color of the fountain in the solarium; now this. Does he think I don't know meanness when I see it?

I raise my eyebrows unencouragingly.

At the party! Remember? I gave you a flyer? His tone is carefully unreproachful.

I thought it was next week, I lie.

WELL SPOUSE SUPPORT GROUP
HOLIDAY GET-TOGETHER!!!

Bring Your Spouse! Wheelchairs Welcome!

Where??? The Melmans
When??? Tuesday, December 5

At the bottom, preceded by a pointing finger, is an inspirational quote (all Well Spouse flyers have inspirational quotes). "I get up. I walk. I fall down. MEANWHILE . . . I keep dancing." —Rabbi Hillel.

Oh, yeah? I think, and write, underneath it, something my lover said yesterday. "Too long a sacrifice makes a stone of the heart." — William Butler Yeats.

I fold the bright-green paper and write Mel's name on it and leave it for Annie, the charge nurse, to give him in the morning. *You won't get me, not that way.*

What I am: teacher of English as a Second Language (ESL), wife (W), mother (M), grandmother (GRM), lover (L). What I am not: Well Spouse (WS). But the undertow grows stronger every day.

Date: December 4, 1999
From: graywolf@hotmail.com
To: lioness@earthlink.net
Subject: delight

Gorgeous desire 4 yesss ssss   dec 8 in nyc
is what im working on with difficulty as to hotel
(ideas) maybe joe will help   magic flute okay
with you?   wear something that shows your
beautiful arms and under it nothing too difficult
so that if iwant you urgently it wont take too
long   you are the bold girl ive always dreamed
of gorgeous lover soon to be against my body head
to head foot to foot even if we were to need it for
any reason ass to ass

Rain by the nightful. Eerie warm December rain. Forsythia was blooming in the New York Botanical Garden, confused into April by the unseasonable temperatures.

Time for more radical measures, Doctor Jacques decrees on our third visit. (His look makes my fingers go to the iris-colored mark Matthew left on my neck. What shows on my face—guilt, or joy?) First, a cystoscopy. *Am I glad I don't have a penis!* Then—he beams, wide, pale face shining like a headlamp, clearly he is *vraiment* 'appy to tell me this—a new technique: they microwave the prostate.

. . . .

My grandson, who is just four, can pee standing up now. He makes us all watch. Often he is called to this task, joyously, in the middle of Sunday dinner.

When I get to the hospital on yet another blue-and-gold afternoon—late, because I gave in to the temptation to bike through Swan Point Cemetery on the path along the Blackstone River—the occupational therapist (OT) is teaching my husband how to fall. Daniel lifts his head to look at me. Where *were* you? his eyes ask. You'd think falling lessons would be the province of the physical therapist (PT), but maybe the doctors see falling as an occupation for Daniel now. "Occupation: Gimp," I saw him write last month on the application for Long-Term Disability (LTD). How sad his large body looks, on all fours, head swinging from side to side with the shame of it. I should not, not, not be thinking of the weekend in New York with Matthew, the wide bed, the gilt-framed mirror, two lithe bodies bending.

Daniel's roommate, on a bedpan, watches with interest. The OT (Chris? Phil?) looks about twelve, shiny with optimism, asking to be quashed. Learning fast, he says; he's my star pupil—aren't you, Teach? Once my husband masters these simple techniques, Chris/Phil tells me, he'll be able to fall without breaking a hip. *Don't they tell you people what a patient's prognosis is?* Once he's in a wheelchair, his neurologist says—and that may be soon—he'll never leave it. Meanwhile, he'll still be able (with my help) to pull himself upright. Meanwhile, I won't have to call the fire department every time he hits the ground.

I watch for a while, poor Daniel first on his nose, then on his knees. The OT rolls up the sleeves of his blue workshirt to reveal muscular young forearms. A nurse I haven't seen before pokes her head around the doorway and cries to Daniel's roommate, No poop in the pooper? Daniel shoots me a glance that says, Leave! and I do.

Passing me in the corridor, Annie, the charge nurse—Daniel's favorite—smiles approval. So faithful, she says, here every day. By the river, when I stopped my bike to rest, beaky black rocks glittered; I found a discarded snake skin hanging from an oak tree. Amazed, enchanted, I brought it to show Daniel, forgetting he's no longer interested in any manifestations of Nature save his own. Now the pale ochre skin, light and shivery and cool, crackles between my palms when I crush it. It drifts to the floor of the hospital corridor like ash.

The sound of a body falling is unmistakable, like no other. Soft yet heavy: a dark sound. The whole house quivers in response, like a campanile to its bell. Whenever I dream of Daniel falling, this sound wakes me. The feel of it in my body, like my own heart beating.

Date: December 9, 1999
From: graywolf@hotmail.com
To: lioness@earthlink.net
Subject: e[ternally your] male

darling lover i was so impatient for you so turned
inside out wanting you im not sure ididnt take
away some of your beautiful flesh in my predatory
mouth   ihave slow sweet designs on your
breasts your cunt your toes and consolation
ihope for your difficult situation these days   my
birthday a warm & fine day but some sense of
amputation with the minus of you   tomorrow
ill try to console you take the best care of your
beautiful (startlingly beautiful it was like seeing
you for the first time yesterday) body & equally
beautiful soul

· · · ·

Lucy knows all sorts of things:

- the give of linoleum versus carpet beneath paper hospital slippers
- the burble of fish in their violet-lighted tank beside the nurses' station
- the changing air: cinnamon rolls, Lysol, urine (ah! urine), the yellow smell of shit

So even though she must hold Mel's hand—which sometimes drags at hers impatiently, sometimes (more cruelly) lets it drop—she has her own experience of this place. I know, because I've just walked blindfolded along the second-floor corridor, sat blindfolded in the solarium. The nurses, who in fact don't like me much, are impressed: they think I'm preparing for my husband's next symptom. What great gulping empathy they attribute to Well Spouses. Where do they get such a view of human nature?

Mel would never do this; he stays resolutely outside Lucy's experience, her pain, as (he told me yesterday) an effective caregiver must. Is that why I did it—to prove I'm not Mel? Or as a penance for the joy I felt last night with Matthew? Or to remind myself where I really live? I don't know. Every day I don't know more (which is not the same thing as knowing, every day, less).

Daniel was an optimistic child, always waiting for something to happen. Outdoors he'd make a nest in the roots of a maple, then stare upward for whole afternoons. Under a shawl of dead leaves he'd trace the bones of birds until the cold drove him inside. Bedtimes, when night rubbed against his windows, he always heard it mentioning tomorrow.

· · · ·

Date: December 12, 1999

From: graywolf@hotmail.com

To: lioness@earthlink.net

Subject: just to reiterate

lover not only is the stain evident on the chair the
blinds are still down and if you are half crazy like me
you can discover our scent still on the seat, iwant
us to be in YOUR office like that too, soon, butter-
fly thigh   coming into you from below was like a
welling over really unexpected & quiet of love and
sex and longing and relief   you did we did nothing
special to make it happen it just could not be held
any longer what belongs to you belongs to you

Zere are two kind of woman. Zee kind which divorce zee 'andicapped,
and zee kind which marree zem.

Last week his neurologist told
me to bring Daniel a book of
crossword puzzles graded easy,
medium, and hard, and have
him do one a day. This afternoon
he shows the first one to me with
a sidelong look.

	35 I	T	E	M
37 T	38 I	D	E	S
41 U		E		
46 S	C	A	R	
49 C	U	N	T	

The brain is part of the spinal cord—we forget that. Conveniently
(Daniel used to tell his graduate students) for our insistence on our
uniqueness among animals. CUNT. What does he know or guess about
my other life? He gazes steadfastly at the opposite wall, where a bulletin

board sports a border of bluebirds around the list of today's activities: Bingo, Chapel, Memory Book.

We're sitting at one of the long tables in the solarium while Mel and Lucy work a puzzle at the other, and the golden afternoon, outside the window, wanes. In a far corner is the German woman, Lotte; her wheelchair glitters in the sunlight. Every now and then she moans, I *vant* to go *home*. The four of us ignore her, having learned from experience that concern invites cursing, spitting, even (if you get close enough) a punch.

Be good! Mel chirps at Lucy, in parting.

She smiles. Not if I get a better offer.

Another flyer has appeared, courtesy of Mel, on the bulletin board in the solarium.

!NEW! W. S. Support Groups !NEW!

WARWICK, RI (KENT HOSPITAL):
Catherine, 401/538-2983

WALTHAM, MA:
Jim Deschenes, 617/551-7037

MANSFIELD, MA
Bea Renzi, 508/697-1715

*"Remember that everything has God's fingerprints
on it."* — *Richard Carlson*

A quick glance around the empty room. Then I add, in red ink, at the bottom:

"In some primitive cultures women are encouraged to practice fellatio, for the protein—especially when nursing."— Margaret Mead

Date: December 15, 1999
From: graywolf@hotmail.com
To: lioness@earthlink.net
Subject: together

i meant it last night & iwill always mean it
we should we must be TOGETHER   iwish you
wanted to hear this but even if you don't the
creeps & voyeurs probably do and anyway ihave to
say it

. . . .

Pickerel Slough, Wisconsin. A hot, bright day. Ahead of us, that bend in the river, like Monet's paintings of the Seine. Our rowboat rocked between wooded banks, the only movement besides the black glitter of gnats, the red wing of a bird deep in the oak trees. We could hear the far-off barking of an axe, and the shadowed water pulsed with quick, bright fish. Daniel propped his rod on the gunwale and began to hum "Blue Room," putting in the trumpet riffs. Silky strands from the willows brushed our faces. On either bank: wild roses, dogwood, white birches, honeysuckle. A sky with thin clouds—peach, mauve, maize— like the inside of a baby's ear. Looks like rain, Daniel murmured.

There is, in any love, a stretch (like the river just before it turns) when perfect happiness is possible. We seized it, he and I. Why is that now no protection? The scent of roses stalks me; the sound of rain on our tent beneath the branches of an oak tree sings like our two bodies.

At the Stop & Shop I ram my cart into the cart of a woman smoking, flagrantly blowing lazy blue signals into the air above the avocados, making people cough. I back up and ram her again. The manager (round young-old face, chestnut hair) is summoned. *Press charges! Go ahead.*

But I am merely asked to leave the store and not to return.

Together, Matthew says. Together? How can we ever be that, when I am already *together*, with Daniel?

When we were young, my husband planned his death: a sailboat turned in the direction of Bermuda with no food on board, sunrise, a tape of Thelonious Monk.

Date: December 17, 1999
From: graywolf@hotmail.com
To: lioness@earthlink.net
Subject: whats wrong

hi heres your e male again   can i say im nervous
that maybe isaid or did something wrong since i
have not heard from you for 3 days now

Sunlight pours through the glass, splashes over the table, the jigsaw puzzle pieces, Lucy's hands. How welcome it would be in a world of snow and ice, a normal mid-December! As it is, outside the long windows buds already deck the branches of the sycamores: tender, red, swollen. Sexual. But of course Lucy, her surprisingly strong-looking hands moving among the puzzle pieces, is unaware of this.

I should not, not, not be thinking of this joke:

> Q: How did Helen Keller burn her hand?
> A: Reading a waffle iron.

Lotte dozes in her wheelchair at the far end of the room, mercifully silent. Daniel and I are playing Scrabble. Keeps the brain alive, the MS newsletter said, but I doubt they had anything like this in mind:

D
EAR
I
MAX
TENOR
N

I put an H on one end of EAR, a T on the other. And my own heart? Is elsewhere, is a tarry lump of resentment and longing.

Daniel plays slowly (I've long since thrown away the little hourglass that times each turn), so I have plenty of time to watch Mel help Lucy with her puzzle—a country landscape—composed of different textures, specially designed for what Mel calls the Visually Impaired. He sits sideways next to her, in dark-red rubbery-looking slacks, with his legs debonairly crossed. As usual he looks not merely cheerful but happy. How does it feel—to know that your affliction is the source of so much joy? Lucy's fingers interrogate each piece. Her expression reminds me of Daniel, three decades ago, gutting fish at our camp on

Pickerel Slough, a hand thrust inside the cold, slick body, rifling its unseen darkness. Quietly, Mel picks up the piece that would fit the spot she's working on, slips it into his pants pocket.

My indrawn breath makes him look at me. Not shame. It's a look of—yes—complicity. The corners of my mouth turn down in revulsion, but he doesn't look away. His shiny little eyes deny my denial.

Lucy yawns. Mel carols, SOMEbody's SLEEPy!

Daniel sits back in a gust of glee. He's covered a triple word score with ZEPER.

Daniel is making progress. In a week or so, Annie, the charge nurse, says, he'll be ready to come home. She hands me a list.

National Family Caregivers Association (NFCA)
1-800-896-3650
www.nfcacares.org

Well Spouse Foundation (WSF)
1-800-838-0879
www.wellspouse.org

Caregivers
847-823-0639
www.caregiving.com

My third-grade teacher made us study snow. We ran in fours out into the cold, each group carrying a large cloth, a kid at each corner, the way firemen hold a net for people to jump into from a burning building. Wisconsin winter air, dry and sparkling, ringing in my lungs, thumping my breastbone. The playground slick with fast-increasing white, and in the margins, a wall of white-sugared stones. No birds except the hardy, songless chickadees. Toes burning with cold inside heavy boots, mittened fingers clumsy as sausages. Snow fell slowly onto the dark-green baize, each flake a heartbeat.

Date: December 19, 1999
From: graywolf@hotmail.com
To: lioness@earthlink.net
Subject: abject

hey darling gorgeous lover I have a lot of things iwant to say to you but the main thing is i love you I LOVE YOU and all the thinking ive been doing about how discouraging and difficult it seems (i am still depressed from our fight which contributes) seems to circle back toward images i cant deny like your teeth biting my tongue your thighs sliding wet on mine   you are wrong to end us WRONG & YOU KNOW IT.

Warm, unseasonable rain coats the city. Taillights gleam in the early evening dark.

The wheelchair feels like a huge heavy stroller. After ten minutes my shoulders ache. I push my husband past the nurses' station, past the zigzagging fish in their fluorescent tank. It's tricky, those vulnerable knees protruding so far ahead. He won't leave this wheelchair, ever. So many losses, and the one thing I'm sure of now is that I can't add another. Holding my breath against the occasional acrid whiff of pee, I thread our way down the corridor between the parked wheelchairs of less lucky patients, the unvisited. They're out here every evening, even the ones who look comatose: the nurses think an after-dinner change of scene is good for them. The livelier ones have the look I've begun to see on Daniel's face, a look that burns through you, that says you're lying even when you're not. I keep my eyes on the top of his head with its incipient gleam of baldness, his graying hair carefully combed by the nurses. I can feel the seductive pull of my (relative) youth. Dimmed eyes are drawn upward; white heads swivel. *I know, I know, you were like me once, all of you. I know this but I do not believe it.* We pass the woman who quacks all day; we pass Lotte, tied into her chair tonight and struggling and shouting (I *vant* to go *home!* I *vant* to go *home!*); we pass the very thin man who holds out trembling arms and calls me by his daughter's name. Hilary? Hilary!

You can take our sweet Teach home day after tomorrow, Annie, the charge nurse, told me this afternoon, beaming, proprietary. He's lucky to have such a faithful wife, aren't you, Teach? Vanguard Medical will deliver a wheelchair just like this one. *Why all that practice falling, then? More of Daniel's precious energy wasted.* Mel, who'd been standing near the nurses' station, showed me a brochure for a sort of forklift to get my husband from his bed into his chair. Awesome machine, Annie said. Then she taught me how to give him his injection, a new medication called Something Interferon. Sticking needles into oranges, pricking my own finger. *Will I sleep for a hundred years?* Daniel's eyes met mine above the poised hypodermic, momentarily alive with the knowledge that we can no longer help each other through our very different sorrows.

There's a crash behind us. A nurse emerges from the room we're passing and begins to run. I start to look around, then remember. *Turn the wheelchair, twit, or he can't see.* How heavy it is, how clumsy I am, with this weight that is my life, now. And there at the end of the shining corridor is Lotte, sprawled facedown on the floor. Indignation and fury have bounced her right out of her wheelchair. Excitement sweeps the corridor. Patients twist in their chairs and crane to see; nurses are on the run. Meanwhile, Lotte keeps on howling. I *vant* to go *home!* she cries to the linoleum.

Date: December 23, 1999
From: graywolf@hotmail.com
To: lioness@earthlink.net
Subject:

it is painful not to be in touch with you   in this
not invasive medium may i still say iwant you sad
or happy, angry or tender, your rich sensuous
mind your conflicted soul your beautiful gifted
golden body

Smell of woodsmoke from our campfire. Pickerel bones and orange rinds on a paper plate. My husband asleep beside me, snoring lightly. Sex slowly drying on our skin, essential and crusty, like salt.

The rain turned from a simple downpour to a storm. Rain drove sideways against the heavy canvas of the tent. When I pulled aside the flap, pale-gold moths, hundreds of them, throbbed against the dark mesh screen.

Stalin Dreaming ❁

FOR SAM DRIVER

IN THE FOYER KOLYA PULLS OFF HIS SHOES, BALANCING ON FIRST ONE leg, then the other. He's late. The whole fourth form was kept after school because he, Kolya Rosanov, called Gorbachev a dupe of capitalism. The year might be 1986, said Pavel Vasilievich, the headmaster, but respect had not been thrown out the window. *Perestroika* only went so far.

The flat is gloomy after the rush-hour cheerfulness of the Arbat. Its emptiness seems to reach for him, and he hesitates in the archway. Papa isn't home yet, though it's almost the dinner hour. Silence fills the high-ceilinged main room that should have echoed with the sounds of the television and the samovar and the girlish telephone chatter of Larissa, his stepmother. When Kolya shaved his head—that was when she moved out. At first he thought that was *why* she moved out, and he couldn't understand it, because didn't she totally agree with him about the necessity for protest, about the responsibility of the individual? Unlike his father, whose motto was, Don't draw attention. Then Larissa told them she'd applied for an exit visa. She wasn't only leaving them; she was leaving the country.

That was two months ago, time enough (his father says) to get used to the new state of things. The room in front of him, for example, dark except for the gray glow of streetlamps through the curtains. Fourteen is too old to miss one's mother—even a stepmother. Kolya makes himself take a step forward, then another.

In the vestibule of the Tretyakov Gallery, Aleksandr Rosanov holds his Burberry across the coat-check counter. The old woman takes it, turns away to hang it on one of the pegs behind her, then turns and thrusts it back at him.

He's late. Golanpolsky is no doubt waiting in the Portrait Gallery, one foot tapping the parquet floor, while Kolya waits at home, alone and dinnerless. But twenty years as a photographer have taught Rosanov patience. He holds the coat out again, letting the woman see the stumps, the remains of his two middle fingers on his left hand. Maybe she'll think he's a veteran. She shakes her head reproachfully, then folds back the collar of his coat to show him the braided leather loop has come undone. *Garderobchiki* refuse all garments lacking loops: every schoolchild knows this. She smiles up at him—smirks, really—revealing a gold tooth flanked by yellowed stumps. *Perestroika* be damned; nothing in *her* world has changed. "*Chort!*" he mutters. The hell with it. His head has suddenly filled with Larissa's coats—hooded sweatshirt, winter *shuba*, precious lambskin jacket he brought back from his assignment in Bonn last spring—all loopless. How Larissa enjoys a confrontation with any government employee, even the lowliest, even *garderobchiki*. It is—*was*—one of the bonds between her and Kolya. Rosanov turns, flinging the Burberry over one shoulder, and strides away.

The Portrait Gallery is deserted at this hour, half past five on a Tuesday. Steam radiators clank in the corners; the room smells of varnish and mice. Its dingy cream-colored walls are hung floor-to-ceiling with paintings of various sizes in heavy, ornate frames. How many pairs of painted eyes? Rosanov feels like the observed rather than the observer, even before Golanpolsky turns around.

"Sasha, my friend! You are late."

Golanpolsky's small bright-brown eyes regard him with sympathy. He is deeply, almost gruesomely, tanned, from a month at a government spa on the Baltic. With his narrow face, all nose, and his pointed black beard, he looks like a compassionate chipmunk.

Rosanov says, "I was held up. Sorry. What was it you wanted?"

Golanpolsky links arms with him and leads him to the largest painting in the room, which has a wall to itself. They stand in front of it as if in contemplation. A boy about Kolya's age sits cross-legged on a grassy promontory, chin resting on his palm in thought, a cloud-streaked sky and some low mountains spread mistily behind him. Boys! Rosanov thinks. Will I never have one minute free of boys?

In English, Golanpolsky says, "The photographs from your . . . ah, your vacation . . . in Azerbaijan pleased our friends very much." His eyes gleam in sardonic amusement at the cloak-and-dagger dialogue. *Irony is not a Russian trait,* Rosanov's mother-in-law—the first one, Kolya's grandmother—likes to say. Golanpolsky, like Larissa, is Jewish.

Rosanov shrugs. As the best medical photographer currently working in the Soviet Union, he is periodically involved in these assignments, yet at the same time above them. Rosanov allows himself to be made use of; the KGB allows Rosanov and his family to live their lives more or less unhampered. He's only a consultant; Golanpolsky is the real thing.

Golanpolsky says, still in English, "They would like enlargements. And they wish you to return to the area for more detailed photographs. Shall we say, day after tomorrow?"

Rosanov is in the middle of a three-week course of lectures on operating room photography at the No. 6 clinic on Shchukinskaya Street; another trip to Azerbaijan will take him away for three or four days. Still: Never hesitate, never refuse. The key to peaceful coexistence with the KGB. "Sure thing," he says, and watches Golanpolsky's nostrils flare in distaste at the colloquialism.

"Good." Now that their business has been transacted, Golanpolsky switches to Russian. "Who does not obey, shall not eat—as our friend up there liked to say." He gestures to the painting on the wall behind him. "Sasha, my friend, I'm delighted to say that I am authorized to buy you dinner. How about the Hotel Metropole?"

Rosanov moves closer to read the painting's title. *Stalin Dreaming*. What a nimble imagination the artist must have had, to see Josef Stalin as this sweet, pensive boy. The boy Kolya was, before Larissa moved out. Rosanov sighs. His son, like his mother-in-law, blames him for Larissa's leaving. (Doubly unfair, since they were both angry with him for marrying her in the first place; it took Larissa half their two-year marriage to win them over.) Yes—old Vera Ivanovna now blames him for losing Larissa just as, twelve years ago, she blamed him for the death of her daughter. But Vera Ivanovna would say that Rosanov *needs* guilt. Rosanov who, mounting prints in his studio the week after Galya died, sliced through two of his fingers with a mat knife. Guilt is a friend, a bulwark against helplessness: if I am guilty, then I could have prevented what happened.

"Sasha, my friend. Where are you? Are you already in Azerbaijan? I have offered dinner at the Metropole."

"Peas, peas, and more peas? No, thanks. I need to get home."

Golanpolsky looks at him, two vertical lines of concern appearing between his brows. "You're too much alone, Sasha. Solitude makes bitter tea."

"What a *babushka* you are! Besides, there's Kolya."

The sardonic gleam reappears. "As you wish."

In the vestibule, Golanpolsky stops to retrieve his properly looped overcoat. Then they detour around an old woman kneeling on the Persian carpet. She's crouched over something, her back curved protectively, in a shaft of dusty lamplight. As they pass, Rosanov looks down. The woman's knobby fingers are pulling a needle and thread in and out through a tear in the carpet, drawing its torn edges together. The two men cross the expanse of shining parquet floor to the great carved double doors where, emerging into the blue October darkness, they part.

Kolya ducks away from his grandmother, from her wide palm running inquisitively over his shaved head. He shrugs off his heavy backpack— he's staying for three nights while Papa is in Azerbaijan—and drops it onto the foyer floor.

"*Gospodi!*" she says. "When will you stop this foolishness? Why do your teachers allow it?"

"I told you, Babushka. It's a protest. We're protesting *disinformatsia.*"

He yanks his blue windbreaker open. The ripping sound always makes his grandmother flinch. It gets an even better reaction on the Metro. Ordinary citizens—people without *blat*, people who wear only Soviet-made clothes—have no experience of Velcro.

"*Disinformatsia?* Don't set foot onto my carpet in those shoes. Look—you've left wet leaves all over." His grandmother goes into the bathroom and reappears with a rag and a dustpan, which she thrusts into Kolya's hands.

"Our textbooks, Babushka," he tells her. "History, philosophy. Biology, even. They're full of lies."

On his knees, he peels blood-colored maple leaves and bits of twigs off the wood floor and puts them in the dustpan. He waits for one of Babushka's proverbs about life—she has them (made up on the spot, he suspects) for every eventuality—but she is interested in something else.

"Your stepmother came by yesterday," she says.

Kolya's heart stops, restarts. He arranges his face in an expression of indifference and looks up.

"She left you this." His grandmother pulls a buff-colored envelope out of the pocket of her cardigan.

Kolya wipes his wet hands on the back of his jeans and takes it from her. It's the first communication of any kind in the two months since Larissa moved out. (Freeze-frame of Larissa in the foyer, surrounded by suitcases, looking sadly up at him, Kolya, as she explained. They mustn't see her anymore, he and his father, non-Jews; it must be clear to the authorities that she's broken with them.) Kolya, ostentatiously casual, tucks the envelope into the waistband of his jeans. Good thing today's the day Papa gets home from his trip. Tonight he'll be back in his own room; he'll have some privacy. "That okay?" He nods in the direction of the floor.

"Life is a great teacher"—Babushka's quoting voice—"but unfortunately it kills all of its students. Wipe it dry, Kolyechka, or it won't shine." She turns her back and thumps into the kitchen, her felt house slippers slapping the floor, but he knows by the nickname she isn't really angry. Maybe she steamed open the letter before she gave it to him—he's seen her do this more than once—which means, until he can get out of here and find a place to read it in private, she knows more than he does. He hates that.

Swiping the rag across the parquet, he goes over, for the thousandth time, the *why* of Larissa's leaving. For decades—since before he, Kolya, was born—practically no one but Jews have been granted exit visas. And even they have to wait months and months, and the minute they apply, they and their families lose everything: jobs, apartments, their places at school. So first Larissa had to divorce him and Papa to show she was completely Jewish. Now she has to wait for clearance. Kolya figures this will take even longer than usual because Papa (as Kolya supposedly does not know) works for the KGB. Right now, for instance, the reason he's in Azerbaijan (Kolya supposedly does not know this, either) is that a secret trial of some new kind of spacecraft killed a bunch of people. Because of these jobs—because of the knowledge of secrets that goes with them—his father has *blat*. So Kolya goes to the special gymnasium for arts and sciences and wears a blue nylon windbreaker made in Germany. But these same secrets are also why, whenever his father leaves the country, Kolya has to stay behind, as security. They're why Papa and Kolya and Babushka can never get exit visas. Ever.

Except that he, Kolya, has a plan. Nikita Khrushchev had his Five-Year Plans; Nikolai Rosanov has a Five-Month Plan.

After he's emptied the dustpan into the toilet and put it in its place underneath the claw-foot bathtub and hung the rag on the tub's edge, Kolya goes into the kitchen. His grandmother has set out glasses of steaming China tea and a bowl of sugar lumps. A plate of sliced apples and cucumbers sits in the center of the table.

"I'm done," he says.

"Good."

They sit down at the scrubbed wooden table, as they do every afternoon when Papa is away and Kolya stays with Babushka. When she's in the mood she tells stories. Sometimes she tells him about his mother, things she said or did as a child, a young girl, but she died before Kolya was two, and these always feel like stories about a stranger. If he has to listen, he'd rather hear about Babushka's childhood—she remembers seeing the young Tsarevich with his sisters, all in white; she remembers long, light summer evenings on the veranda of her father's *dacha* on the Black Sea—or about the siege of Stalingrad, and Babushka running the blockade, and how her older sister died of starvation. Lucky for him, he takes after his grandmother and not after Papa. He, Kolya, isn't afraid to draw attention. He, Kolya, acts. *The future is not his who obeys*—Babushka says it herself.

But this is one of her silent afternoons. The two of them sip the hot, fragrant tea through sugar lumps clenched between their teeth, and look out the window. In Kolya's waistband the letter from Larissa crackles when he moves. He thinks of the Plan, a peculiar sensation in his chest, as if his heart had the hiccups. *Tomorrow is also a day.* The lowering sun gilds every window in the apartment house opposite, and now and then the shadows of migrating birds flow across its gray concrete wall.

Rosanov, back in Moscow and swaddled in jet lag, shoves his way through the crowd at the *rynok*, checking off items on his list. A chicken, cooked and jointed; potatoes; onions; beets. There's nothing to eat in the flat. Kolya will return from his grandmother's at six o'clock, his usual impassive, sullenly ravenous self. Ahead lies another evening of morose male silence. Kolya will hunch over his homework, lips moving occasionally to caress the more difficult English consonants; Rosanov will go through the proofs his students turned in before he left for Azerbaijan. Eventually he'll get up and put a record on the stereo, maybe (braving his son's scorn) Bach.

In Azerbaijan—warm, beautiful, dotted with the ruins of the great prison camps—Rosanov dreamed as he hadn't dreamed in years. He was made of ground meat, packed into the shape of a man, and crumbled away when touched. He was undressing Galya, his first wife, two months pregnant with the baby who was never born, and the veins in her breasts became slender strings of sapphires. Awakened by the sound of thunder, he lay and listened to the rattle of rain on the window glass, waiting for the flashes of lightning that felt somehow celebratory in the mild darkness. Children dream more than adults, he read somewhere; the fetus dreams almost constantly. Maybe Sirvan, his Azerbaijani assistant, was right, and crossing time zones makes you momentarily younger? The dreams' content Rosanov refuses to ponder. He's never liked taking autopsy photographs, hates the salty smell of morgues, their bleak, premonitory lighting.

Apples. Carrots. Kolya. Why can't his son find a passion, whatever the thing is that will make him invest himself, give him a future, a plan? Rosanov was fifteen when his father gave him his first camera, a Brownie box camera procured God knew how. No film to be had then, in 1957. But even without being able to take a single picture, he knew. For three years, until he entered the university, Sasha Rosanov carried that camera everywhere, slouched all over Moscow with it buttoned inside his jacket.

Women walk toward him carrying string bags full of—yes, it really *is*—oranges. Some as small as tennis balls, some as large as grapefruit. Rosanov imagines Kolya's eyes widening in surprise when he brings them home. But when he investigates, he sees that the line for such a rarity extends out the rear entrance of the *rynok* and down the block to Leninsky Prospekt. He goes back inside to the stalls of ordinary fruits and root vegetables. A young woman with a Baltic accent and a mustache hands him half-a-dozen fat mushrooms in a brown paper cone, along with a look of mixed suspicion and pity—men do not shop for food, unless they're pensioners—and takes his five-ruble note. Rosanov turns away without waiting for his change and stalks off toward the bakery. When will he stop wearing the stigma—invisible to him but apparently all too clear to others—of a man whose wife has left him? He has to fight the urge to seize perfect strangers by the lapels and spit the truth into their faces. *I didn't lose her—I freed her.*

He goes about the rest of his errands in the cold October afternoon, a light, not-yet-serious snow swirling around him like smoke. At

Sheremetyevo he does not find waiting for him the supplies he ordered from Helsinki. This is his second trip to the airport in less than twenty-four hours, if he counts his arrival from Azerbaijan at midnight. The E-6 chemicals and slide mounts (in Azerbaijan he had to develop his own film on-site) can wait until Golanpolsky sends him on another field trip, but he urgently needs neutral-density filters for the too-bright light in the No. 6 clinic's operating room, not to mention three Norman strobes to replace the ones his assistant broke. As he stands in line at the post office, his last stop, he is still thinking about Larissa. She isn't ungenerous — just one of those people who somehow always get more than they give. And really isn't he more to blame for the way things went, being older and what passes for wiser — being aware of the existence of a trade? He knew when they married that his connections, his influence, were a big part of what attracted her. *Blat!* It should have occurred to him this very thing might one day become a liability. *The source of a spring,* Vera Ivanovna, his mother-in-law, would say, *is also its limit.*

A wiry old woman, bent as a coathanger, scuttles up to him. In the whining baby talk of *babushkas,* she says, "Won't you give me, dear little son, a tiny little glass of water?" Rosanov shakes his head and turns away. Then a strange thing happens. When he glances back, the old woman's face has become Larissa's: straight brows, dark eyes, small, determined chin. A face he hasn't seen since she moved out. He flinches, but when he opens his eyes, it's just an old woman again. She has to twist her neck at what seems like a painful angle in order to look up at him. He finds himself saying, in the same antique baby talk, "Very well, little mother." He follows her across the marble floor to the water tap, reaches for the metal cup chained to the spigot, fills it and holds it out to her. She seizes the cup. Then, before he can withdraw his hand, she kisses the two shiny stumps of his fingers. Hastily letting go, he turns and walks quickly toward the door.

By the time Rosanov reaches the flat, a sludgy darkness has fallen.

He's so loaded down he can't reach his keys. At his knock, Kolya opens the door and stands back. Rosanov sees disappointment on his face. He thrusts the string bag full of brown-paper-wrapped purchases into his arms. "Put these away." The sum of the day's irritations hardens his voice. "And put some water on to boil, for the potatoes," he says to Kolya's departing back.

Kolya turns around. For an instant, a half-heartbeat, his face is full of hate. He stretches out his arm. The string bag hangs from his hand, its weight shifting so that it sways slightly.

"Boil it yourself," he says.

Then he throws the bag. Not at Rosanov—not quite. It hits the row of coats on the wall next to him and falls with a loud thud onto the floor. Kolya stands looking at it for several seconds, transfixed. Then he turns and walks, slowly, deliberately, down the hall to his room. The door shuts behind him with a click.

Rosanov, who hasn't moved or spoken, hangs his coat on its hook and exchanges his shoes for felt house slippers. In the living room he searches the shelves above the phonograph for the recording of the *Saint Matthew Passion* he bought in Bonn last spring. Before Larissa announced she was leaving; before his son turned into Kolya the Indifferent, Kolya of the Slouch. Rosanov lowers the needle carefully onto the spinning black disk, then sits down on the couch. A tenor voice sings, *Let my heart be pure as Thine.* He hears Kolya leave his room and go into the foyer, then the rustle of paper wrappings. *There a precious grave I'll make Thee.* He should be angry; instead, he feels like one of the longitudinal split stills his students are learning how to make. Half of him relieved (signs of life in Kolya); the other half, afraid (Kolya out of control, winding up in an iron leg cuff, chained to a bench in the Gorky Street police station). After ten minutes or so, there are footsteps down the hall and into the kitchen, the sound of water running into the big iron kettle. Better, surely, not to make an issue of what happened just now? It's been hard on the boy having Larissa leave so suddenly, so completely. Even if she *was* more like a mischievous older cousin than a stepmother.

Rosanov leans back and closes his eyes. The music bathes him in warmth, in light. He thinks wistfully of the last few nights in Azerbaijan: late suppers in a smoke-filled café, with laughter (off-color jokes in the morgue staff's blend of Russian, Armenian, and Georgian) in his ears and the heat of vodka in his stomach and watermelon juice running down his chin.

Larissa's letter is their special kind, the kind they used to leave for each other in one of the kitchen cupboards behind a loose board—the place spies in movies call the "drop." Larissa's idea, intended (Kolya supposedly did not know) to win him over and make fun of Papa at the same time. (Freeze-frame of Larissa glancing at him over the shiny cover of her magazine, smiling her little tucked-in smile: *Our secret, Kolya.*) They used to cut words and phrases out of the old English-language magazines Papa brought home and paste them onto notepaper.

He's reading the words for the tenth time since dinner; they keep sliding away as if written on water. The Plan, he reminds himself, then looks up in alarm. But Papa just sits there looking at his stupid proofs, photographs of blood-soaked guts and hacked-off legs and deformed babies, and listening to his stupid Bach. Kolya folds the note into quarters. He tucks it back inside his English grammar.

"THE WORLD'S MOST EXPERIENCE." He remembers the exact ad the phrase comes from. "Fly Pan Am . . . The World's Most Experienced Airline." So Larissa *does* want him to come with her. That means he must be included on her exit visa—the one piece of the Plan he hasn't firmed up yet. Because for two whole months he's kept his promise. For two whole months he hasn't gone to the flat on Vavilova Street where Larissa lives with her mother and brother. Near it, but not *to* it. Now, now he'll see her.

He'll have to act sooner than he planned, though. Tomorrow he'll (1) Take the Metro to Leninsky Prospekt, then the No. 33 bus to Vavilova; (2) Show Larissa how much English he's learned since she left; (3) Demand—no, *agree*—to go with her to Tel Aviv.

The next day—the last day of October—Rosanov strides along Kutuzovsky Prospekt in the syrupy golden light. Indian summer, he remembers, is the American name for this sudden, brief, deceptive reprise. The weather Russians call *Bab'e Leto*: "Summer of Women." The late afternoon air is fizzy and tickling. He turns north onto Tchaikovsky Street toward the American Embassy.

And here is Golanpolsky, alighting from the tram, coatless (he grew up, or so he says, in Novosibirsk) and smiling. Rosanov feels a minor rush of gladness. Could it be Golanpolsky is the closest thing he has to a friend these days? When his first wife died, the friends of his single years returned to him; when he remarried, they once again melted away. He loved Larissa's tartness, her femaleness that was not soft but wiry and vigilant. It seemed like—it *was*—enough.

Now, though, Golanpolsky—who since the divorce seems to have adopted him—has decided it's time for a change. Has procured for Rosanov an invitation to the American ambassador's autumn reception, which several members of the KGB hierarchy attend every year. ("Don't be naïve, Sasha, my friend," he said, when Rosanov expressed surprise at this. "Their spies, our spies. We are all in the same line of work.")

They show their heavy, cream-colored invitations to one of the marines in the archway, wait for his nod, then pass between another pair of marines through the door into the vestibule. Golanpolsky smoothes his little pointed beard in the mirror beside the coat-check while Rosanov waits behind him. "Life is divided into three periods," Golanpolsky tells his reflection. "The premonition of love, the action of love, and the recollection of love." He turns away with a satisfied air. "Now, Sasha, my friend. There's someone I'd like you to meet."

He lays an arm across Rosanov's shoulders as they go up the stairs to the reception room. "Another day, two at the most—then we'll see true winter. Six months of it," he says, with relish.

Kolya can feel his heart beating. His knuckles graze Larissa's door— too soft. *Chort!* He pounds, then waits. Nothing. He knocks again. There's a small sound—sharp, like buckshot—from the door of the flat across the hall—the wooden cover being pushed back from its peephole.

Maybe Larissa and her mother and her brother are all out? Kolya leans against the cold, dirty wall, prepared to wait.

The door across from him opens slightly. A face appears in the crack. A voice, a woman's, says, "They've gone. Left on Monday." The face withdraws; the door closes.

Kolya eases his backpack off and lets it drop. He shoves both hands into the pockets of his black leather jacket and slides down the wall until his butt hits the floor. The woman lied. Larissa wouldn't leave without him. He gazes evilly at the door of the other flat through half-closed eyes. *Life is not a spectacle*—Babushka's voice—*it is a predicament.* The hallway stinks: pee, ancient cooking, the smell of rats, like old tires. Minutes pass, punctuated by an occasional small scuffling sound. He thinks it's about five, but he isn't sure. He sold his watch, along with his CDs and the American jeans Papa gave him at New Year's, in preparation for departure. He could have gotten twice as much for the jacket, brought back by Papa from Bonn, but it's just right for the mild winter breeze off the Red Sea.

There's the sound of the peephole cover again from the door opposite. Closed; open. Kolya imagines the eye behind it, pressed against the cold glass. Imagines peeling the eyeball like a boiled egg. Glistening veins exposed and writhing across its raw red surface, like one of Papa's photos. *Chort! Call the Authorities!* But he knows they won't. They're afraid of him, of his noise; afraid he'll draw attention, get them noticed, get them in trouble. He gazes up at the peephole, unblinking, beaming this knowledge toward it with steady malevolence.

More time passes. Kolya doesn't know how long. Maybe he even nodded off, because he has a sudden sharp apprehension of emptiness. This is followed by a feeling more terrible than anything he's ever known. For a second he thinks, I'm dying. He can't stay still a moment longer.

He's knocking—pounding—on Larissa's door. The peephole in the door opposite snaps open.

And then he's kicking it, Larissa's door, the thud of his heavy boots resounding in the empty hallway. How could she leave without him? "*Chort!*" he shouts.

The door opposite opens. He keeps on kicking. Finds a rhythm.

How *could* she? How *could* she? Glimpse of a figure in the corner of his eye. The wood of Larissa's door splinters against his boots, his toes inside them burning with pain. A woman's voice cries, "*Oy! Gospodi!*"

Let them look. Let them see the fucking future. He is kicking it. He's kicking everything. Pavel Vasilievich and all the other teachers. Gorbachev. Papa. Larissa. He's kicking *life*, kicking the shit out of it.

Pleasantly tipsy, as much from the low pink moon (a "worm moon," Galya used to call it) and the softness of the night air as from the American Embassy's abundant single-malt scotch, Rosanov has to search for his key. His head is filled with the pleasures of the evening just passed. The water luminous in the blue night as he crossed the bridge over the Moskva, the tanker downstream with its flag of pure white smoke, the moon. The woman at the reception. The remarkable woman whom Golanpolsky introduced him to. American, tall, slender, with dark hair that curled around her face in petals, like a chrysanthemum, and clear eyes oddly light against her smooth, tanned skin. Thinking of her, Rosanov turns his key the wrong way in the lock. When he reverses it, and the door opens, the flat is dark. Maybe Kolya's decided to sleep at his grandmother's? Rosanov feels a small, shameful twinge of relief: the evening to himself, his mood unmarred, a little Bach. A little time to think about the woman's eyes.

But no: there he is — a dark, hunched form in a corner of the divan, outlined in dusty light from the windows overlooking the Arbat.

"Kolya?"

Silence, but the dark form shifts a little. Rosanov switches on a lamp. Kolya turns his face away. "Don't!"

"What is it?" Rosanov asks, knowing he shouldn't. "Kolyechka! What's the matter?"

Moving slowly, carefully, he sits down on the other end of the divan. Kolya says nothing, but he doesn't move away, either. He still has his jacket on, his prized leather jacket (*Something* I've done right, Rosanov thinks), though his boots and socks are lying on the rug in front of him. Rosanov looks down at his son's bare feet. They're puffy and red, beginning to bruise. The big toe on his left foot is bleeding.

"What happened?" Rosanov says again. His mother-in-law's question: *What has come to you—joy, or sorrow?*

"Nothing."

"Have you eaten?"

Kolya shrugs.

Rosanov regards the back of his son's head for a few seconds, then extends an arm along the top of the sofa, stealthily, until his fingers graze his son's shoulder. Kolya turns to look at him. His face is terrifying in its grief. He turns away again—it's over in an instant—but Rosanov feels as if a hand has squeezed his heart.

This is not the boy he knows.

It takes all Rosanov's strength, all his determination, to sit still. He wants to put both arms around his slumping son, to seize him, hold him. As if that would make this unknown boy familiar again. But somehow he understands that this boy would hate that. Hate to know he's been *seen*.

After a few minutes, helplessness drives Rosanov to his feet. He goes into the kitchen and opens the refrigerator. He chips ice off the inside of the freezer compartment with a screwdriver, grateful for the simplicity of this, for the need to strike something. He finds a clean, frayed towel to put the ice in, and a soft cloth, and fills a bowl with warm water. He finds a roll of gauze and some tape and a blue glass bottle of antiseptic. But what can he offer his son? Too young for the consolation of vodka, too old to be comforted by hot milk and honey. In the cupboard above the sink he finds only some stale biscuits, some black currant jelly, a jar of Tang bought God-knows-how-long-ago in some airport duty-free shop. As a child Kolya loved to eat it straight out of the jar. Rosanov's hand closes around it. He takes two spoons out of the drawer. He finds the lacquered tray with the picture of Saint George and the Dragon and piles onto it the things he has accumulated.

In the main room he sets the tray on the table next to Kolya. Then he turns on the stereo and lowers the needle carefully onto the record. Bach pours into the room. Kolya does not protest when Rosanov kneels in front of him and lifts his feet into his lap, or flinch at the touch of the towel dipped in water. A warm baritone voice sings, *In the evening, when it was cool.* Kolya's blue-jeaned knees are at eye level. They are shaking.

I know, Rosanov would like to say; I know. But it will come—whatever it is that you want so much. You just have to wait, and be ready.

Instead, he keeps his eyes on his work. Between his palms he feels one foot, then the other—bony, long, smelling the way feet smell— pause and tense, like a small animal poised for flight. *In the evening,* the voice sings. Now the antiseptic. This will hurt, he almost says. But this new, unknown boy might resent a warning, might feel his courage impugned. *In the evening . . . evening.* Without speaking, Rosanov swabs clear blue antiseptic lightly over Kolya's toes. The foot he is holding jerks, nearly escapes. Looking up, he sees Kolya catch his lower lip between his teeth, the way Galya used to do. *In the evening the dove returns, an olive leaf in its mouth. O beautiful time! O evening hour!* For some reason, as he winds the gauze around the clean, still bleeding toe, he remembers his son's first word—*owl*—remembers how Galya's face, round with the new pregnancy they'd decided they could not afford, lit with laughter as he said it. *Owl.* Rosanov presses the tape into place. For a second he holds his son's bandaged feet, one in each hand, as if weighing them. Then he sets them gently down.

Sharks ❁

PALE WITH ANTICIPATION, ANNA TUGGED ON MY ARM. "IS IT ALMOST here, Mama?" When I didn't answer instantly, she said, "Mama! Is it almost here?" She would have gone on asking the question over and over until I answered.

"Yes," I said. "Yes. It's almost here."

I looked down at her. The sun struck her dark-blonde braids, uneven ones she'd insisted on making herself. She was wearing a red-and-white parka printed all over with hearts, new since the weekend before last, and a pair of jeans with a roadrunner embroidered in multicolored thread on the hip pocket. Her eyes were red. From the cold, I told myself. The day had the hard brilliance of late fall. Under the golden-leaved maples, where we stood, the sun warmed the air, but it was a warmth with cold at its heart. I put my arm around Anna, but she pulled away.

It's okay, I told myself. Take your time.

Where was that bus? My watch said quarter to ten, more or less: it had no numerals, only little dots where the numbers should have been. A year ago, before John got custody, Anna was learning how to tell time and she looked at my watch one day and burst out crying. What's the matter, I asked her. We were brushing our teeth and her face was a mess of toothpaste foam and tears. There isn't any time, she sobbed. You don't have any time.

The bus came, and we got on. Anna ran to the back while I put our money in the slot and waited for transfers. I forgot to tell the driver she was under six and ended up buying two full fares.

When I sat down, Anna was reading the strip of ads that ran above the windows, her lips moving soundlessly. It was warm in the bus. I pulled my heavy sweater off over my head and unzipped Anna's coat. There were violet smudges under her eyes. John had been waiting with her in front of the apartment when I got home from work at the hospital (he won't come inside anymore, because of Susan), and after I'd fed her and read to her, I tucked her into the wide double bed in our bedroom. Out in the living room, Susan and I heard her sobbing quietly for a few minutes, then silence. I told myself she was overexcited because of the trip to the zoo and the strangeness of staying overnight with me—but really I knew the sound of grief when I heard it. Before Susan and I went to bed, I got Anna and moved her into the sleeping bag in the living room, on top of the sheepskin rug. Her new pajamas, the flannel kind with feet, had a scratchy ring of lace around the wrists and ankles. Her body was heavy and warm.

Anna nudged me. "No what? Mama! No what?"

I followed her gaze. "Deposit," I said. "No Deposit, No Return."

She went back to her silent, careful decoding.

John is very proud of how well his daughter can read. "Marie," he said to me the week before last, in a rare moment of unbending, "she can read *dentifrice!*" She started first grade this fall. She's a different child now, and not only (though I wish I could believe it) because of school. In the year since John and I separated—the year of having an every-other-weekend mother—she's become reserved and watchful.

We had to read every ad in the bus and every sign we saw from the window on the way out of New Brunswick. Anna especially likes No Parking signs. A phrase doesn't lose its charm for her by being repeated.

When I was a child, I used to like to look at houses from the bus, try to see inside them, look at the things in the yards. I'd look down the side streets, imagining where the people came from who waited at the bus stop, how far they'd walked, and where they were going. I was always wanting other lives, then—imagining them, trying to get inside them. Today the people who got on at the local stops all seemed to be smiling, and the lives behind them all seemed like something you'd want.

The bus swept onto the Jersey Turnpike. Anna was silent, chewing on the string of her hood. Lately she chews on everything—the ties at the neck of her dresses, her hair-ribbons, the tails of her stuffed animals. Whatever she's been chewing on looks repulsive afterwards, all gray and stringy.

Finally she said, "Know what happened to Brooke?"

"Who's Brooke?"

"*Brooke*. She just moved into the house next door. She's my best friend."

"What happened to Brooke?" A best friend I didn't even know about.

"She had her independence out."

"She did?" I kept my face straight. Anna had the slightly cross-eyed look she has when she's trying out a new word. She gets really mad now if you laugh at her.

"Yeah. Does it hurt?"

My heart lifted. My daughter was talking to me—really talking to me—for the first time since her father dropped her off last night. I said, in my still-your-mother voice, "Well, probably. A little, anyway."

"But they put you to sleep? Mama? They put you to—"

"Yes," I said.

"And you don't feel anything?"

"Not while you're asleep."

For a moment, her questions—our old rhythm of question and answer, like the call-and-response of birds—gave the old Anna back to me. I held my breath and looked out at the sunny day. It seemed as fragile as a soap bubble, and as bright.

Anyone would say it was my fault that I'd lost her. But isn't watching a child grow up always a long series of losses? The baby, then the toddler, then the small child vanish, one into the next. You miss them; they never come back. They're in there somewhere, though, hidden one inside the other like those little wooden Russian dolls.

Anna shifted in her seat, moving just a little closer to me. "You could stay asleep forever," she said. "Sharks sleep with their eyes open. In the Gulf of Mexico."

I pictured the green ocean-bottom twilight, the sharks sleeping wide-eyed in the watery gloom. Hanging there motionless next to each other, asleep but still connected.

"When you wake up, it hurts?" Anna asked.

"What? Oh. When you have an operation, you mean? Yes. A little."

She looked up at me. A few wisps of dark-blonde hair had strayed across her face, and I brushed them away. She said, "I got four stitches in my knee."

"Yes, I know," I said. I was *there*—I thought—don't you remember?

"Want to see?"

"I've already seen them, honeybunch."

I saw her eyes go blank and shuttered, like her father's.

"Hey," I said. "Let's see."

She shrugged—a newly acquired gesture, world-weary and immune. I leaned over and rolled up the leg of her jeans. Her shoelace, I noticed, had come untied.

"That's quite a scar," I said.

But Anna wouldn't look at me.

I unrolled the leg of her jeans and tucked her sock back under it. She held still; she let me. But when I reached for her shoelaces, she brushed my hand away. "I can do it," she said.

She began taking the shoelaces out of her sneakers, then rethreading them. Sunlight slanting through the window fell on the tender back of her neck above her T-shirt. I remembered the exact moment when I knew that I loved her. For the first year of her life I felt as if someone had handed me a puppy or a kitten to take care of. But then came a day, a winter morning, very bright. I remember watching her, sitting in sunshine in the doorway between the kitchen and the living room. The light caught in her hair made it glitter. She was pulling the laces out of her little soft shoes. .

Now the bus changed direction in a long, smooth arc, shifting Anna's weight against me. We were close to the city. The smokestacks of Elizabeth began to poke through the haze, and the bus, slowing down, entered a long arched stone underpass that was a favorite of graffiti artists.

"Eat. Out. At. Dick's," Anna read. Her voice was loud with delight at finding four easy words together. The man across the aisle looked at me sideways out of small bright eyes, like one of Anna's gerbils. Then he smiled, somewhere between a grin and a leer. You jerk, I thought. I glared at him until he looked away.

Jerk.

It's not what people seem to think; it's not that I hate men. But I love Susan now.

Anna finished with her shoelaces and tied the ends into double bows. "At this zoo, do the lions and tigers run around loose? Like at Wildlife Safari?"

"No, honeybunch. It's in the middle of the Bronx."

Anna gave that shrug again, so much older than her years, the shrug that said no disappointment was surprising. She turned away from me and looked out the window. She reached over her shoulder for the end of one of her pigtails and chewed on it.

This winter we're going to make a braided rug. Long winter evenings by the fire—I think Anna must have seen it on "Little House on the Prairie." She loves the idea of making things. Most of what she has her eye on is too hard for her—embroidery and quilting and all that. But a braided rug is something she could do, I think. Something we can do together. Side-by-side, working evenly, calmly, every other Saturday night. A way to stay connected, like the watchful sleep of sharks. She can tie her own shoes and braid her own hair. That's really all there is to it.

The Angel of Entropy ❀

P EOPLE WOULD CHANGE FOR HER. FROM THE AGE OF NINE—THE
March afternoon when potato-pale Philip Schneider had brought
her, from his mother's jewelry box, two golden poodle pins with false
ruby eyes—Claire knew this.

She knew, too, almost as early, to exercise care. She did not want
(not always) the responsibility. She knew she could be too harsh—
whenever her father or her sister, Evvie, got sick, she'd end up telling
them to pull themselves together—but she didn't always know when
she was doing it. It was a fine line she had to walk. Because for Evvie—
who, being so much younger, hadn't really had a mother—Claire had
always had to be strong, to be certain. She thought of it, growing up, as
looking sure.

It wasn't exactly that their father was neglectful, but what he wanted
most, he said often, was for his girls to be self-reliant. It didn't help,
either, that Claire grew too fast. More is expected of a tall child. Like
a forced plant, at eleven she was almost as tall as her father, the tallest
child in the sixth grade, taller than any of the nuns at Saint Ignatius
except Sister Mary Cleophas. Claire didn't know whether her father
loved Evvie more, or just differently. He might even, she came to think
later, when she was in high school, have been compensating for loving
Evvie less. Their mother, after all, had died because of Evvie; she'd had

breast cancer but had gone ahead with the pregnancy anyway. The baby was a burden and a thief who'd cost Daddy the person he loved most in the world.

"The baby's all right—that's a mercy," six-year-old Claire heard a woman say when the squalling loaf-like bundle was exhibited to some neighbors. But she wasn't all right. A scratch on her brain—the lightest and thinnest of fingernail scratches, like a sliver under your skin. *Lesion.* One of the new words Claire learned the next year, the year she was in second grade, along with *symptom, organic, epilepsy.* Another thing she learned: never, ever to hit her sister, never to yell at her, never to lose her temper. *Patience.* Three seizures in succession; then for a long time—more than a decade—nothing.

Plants flower, Claire learned in Botany 101, in her first year at Rhode Island College, because they're going to die soon. At fifteen, Evvie burst into bloom. Fever roses in her cheeks, eyes a deep blue, skin as smooth and unmarked as the petals of gardenias. She shaved half her head, dyed the other half parrot-feather green and wore it standing out stiffly from her head in all directions, like (she said) the Statue of Liberty. "SPIKED FOR SCHOOL," read the caption below her photograph in the *Providence Sun-Times* that September, snapped by a photographer trolling the early-morning bus stops in search of local color. Evvie held her head proudly, precariously: a barbaric princess drowning in her own splendor.

The seizures started again that spring, accompanied by wild mood swings and hallucinations. Hospitals, EEGs, blood work. More words, not new this time but invested with terrible new meaning: *procedure, episode, exacerbation.* Medications with names that sounded like characters in *Star Wars*—Nardil, Klonopin—and side effects that required blood monitoring and complicated dietary restrictions.

Other, later photographs. Evvie in her first (and last) year at the Rhode Island School of Design, wrapped mummy-like from head to foot in toilet paper, a cigar protruding from the lip-level slit. Evvie, plump now from the medications, holding aloft a gallon milk bottle painted black. (In the Baltimore catechism of their childhood, three milk bottles illustrated the soul: the state of grace was a white bottle; venial sin, a bottle with bruises; mortal sin, all black. The photograph commemorated Evvie's lost virginity.) Evvie nude on the pages of *Tattoo International*, exhibiting Claire's friend Julia's largest and most ambitious work, a dark-blue pattern of fronds and ferns covering the left side of Evvie from armpit to knee, stark as a warning against her gleaming, gardenia-pale skin.

It was dangerous to love Evvie. For one thing, she kept the ruth-less innocence of childhood. Her shimmering self-absorption first stunned you, then filled you with longing—with the undeniable flooding realization of all you yourself had lost. That was disorienting enough, but there was more. At seventeen, dismayed by the weight she'd gained and the dismal, logy way she felt, she started going off her meds. Then, frightened by the highs and lows, by the unrecover-able periods of absence the seizures caused, she went back on them. On, off, on again. Off her meds, she was irresistible. Her recklessness captured you. Her meanness (and Evvie could be cruel—Oh! she could) only made her more compelling. No matter how often she stepped over the line between brave and foolhardy, she always came out all right. She sowed chaos wherever she went, but she, Evvie, was fine. A charmed life, people said. But Claire thought (sometimes bitterly) that what kept Evvie safe wasn't luck at all, but the strenu-ous, unceasing, unnoticed efforts of others. *Efforts of mine*, was what Claire meant. Invisible mending.

• • • •

A lurching sun-and-showers spring day. Home early for lunch to wait for the exterminator (her father took Nicholas, her three-year-old son, on the days Claire worked) she found Evvie on the floor watching a silent TV. On the screen, sitting in a high-backed chair before a wall of books, was Claire's ex-husband. Seeing him felt like being punched in the breastbone. Claire stood there while the breath drained out of her, watching. He'd shaved off his mustache; his long shallow upper lip, like a candy scoop, made him look doleful.

"Hey, Claire! It's Vince," said Evvie, unnecessarily. On the floor in front of her was a fan of Day-Glo orange envelopes. Moving awkwardly because her left arm was in a cast from wrist to elbow, she pulled out an envelope and tucked it into another spot, like someone sorting a poker hand. She looked up at Claire, a quick sidelong gleam. "You don't mind, do you?"

Claire had learned long ago not to answer that quick gleam of cruelty. "No," she said, though everything inside her shouted, Turn him off!

She walked slowly across the room to where the TV crouched beneath the huge dirty windows, bars of weak spring sunlight striking her face. On the small screen a grainy, gray Vince mouthed answers to a woman interviewer. Photo-sensitive glasses, as usual, screened his eyes, so you never quite felt you saw him. Your impulse of course was to try harder, get closer; it took a long time to find out you never would. Claire turned up the volume to show Evvie how little she cared.

" — reprehensible." Vince's voice made her stomach thump. "With all the resources at our command today . . . Still the richest country in the . . . One cannot comprehend . . ."

"Oh, turn it off," said Evvie. "What a cheeseball!"

Claire turned the volume knob. Vince's mouth opened and shut

in the mute communication of fish. She pushed the knob in. With a
snap, like a wishbone breaking, Vince vanished. Two and a half years,
she thought, thirty months; that's almost a thousand days since he left.
Will I never get used to it?

"He's a real Adirondack. And I used to think he was cool." Evvie
repositioned another envelope. Above the grimy canvas sling, the nape
of her neck looked white and tender. She must have hennaed her hair
while Claire was at the lab. One loose lock, glowing with inward purple, hung down like a question mark.

"A what? What are you doing?"

"Adirondack. You know—a guy who's high on himself. I'm paying
all my traffic tickets. First I've gotta get them in chronological order.
Why's he even *on* that show in the first place? I thought Vince's thing
was, like, ballet and all that."

"Wherever there's a need, wherever there's a TV camera docu-
menting it, Vincent is there." Cheap; maybe even unjust? A well-
known arts administrator could surely be allowed a mild public passion
for environmental causes. "Can I help?"

There were more orange envelopes scattered over the floor behind
Evvie, along with a copy of *The Smart Job Search* and several changes
of clothing. Wherever Evvie went, disorder bloomed; machines broke
down; objects disappeared. The angel of entropy, their father used to
call her. Patiently, Claire picked her way across jeans, a Harvard sweatshirt, an octopus of lacy bras, and sat down cross-legged next to her
sister.

"You have to go to municipal court when they're overdue like
this," Evvie said. "It's someplace on LaSalle. I'm gonna plead nolo
contendere."

Claire gathered up a handful of envelopes. Trying, as always, to
enter her sister's world. She'd probably be let off with a reduced fine

and a warning: Evvie, the person everyone wanted to be, the one who got away with it. Twenty-three-year-old Evvie, who referred to herself cheerfully as a Jill-of-all-trades, who lived, for the moment, on unemployment. She'd been fired from her job at the SPCA for abducting ("Rescuing, Claire—I *saved* them") two cats scheduled to be put down. No exasperated speech from a worried Claire made a dent in Evvie's satisfaction. She was off her meds again, and impervious. Even breaking her arm—she'd had to jump from the top of the cyclone fence in the dark, holding the cats—hadn't fazed her.

Claire began sorting her envelopes by date. It was hard, the handwriting on most of them a hasty ballpoint scrawl. Evvie laid hers down one by one in the fan on the floor, her cast knocking on the bare wood. Don't bail her out, Julia had advised. Let her learn from her mistakes, the way you let Nicholas. Julia, who'd known Evvie almost as long as she'd known Claire, claimed to understand her. The tattoos, she said, were Evvie's translation of her inner reality—hidden and painful and strange—into something the world could see. They were honorable scars. "She's not spaced out, Claire. She's spaced *in*."

Claire didn't listen. As witness to the fact that Evvie was here at all, living with Claire, having been evicted from her flat in Pawtucket for possession of four cats and an iguana. The loft was crowded and messy with the three of them, and Evvie was probably a bad influence on Nicholas. But what else could I do? Claire asked herself.

A sudden shower made the room grow dim. Claire had to lean back and hold each envelope up to the windows to make out the scribbled dates. The homey smell of pot roast seeped into the room from the hall. Squinting, Claire noticed the entry next to LOCATION on the envelope she was holding. Prospect Street—Vince's street. She held the envelope higher. In the smoky light she made out "Prospect @ Jenckes." Vince's corner. She grabbed more envelopes from the floor, destroying Evvie's careful fan. Two, three, four of them. All the same, "Prospect @ Jenckes." A click, small and solid as tumblers turning in a lock. Something she'd known without knowing, coming to rest. Evvie and Vince.

It was raining heavily now, streaming down the tall windows and coating them with gloom. The bright orange envelopes seemed to be the only color in the room. They pulsed in the watery dimness. Evvie stood up. She was so thin, the way she got when she went off her meds, that she looked breakable. She regarded Claire in silence. That side-long gleam. The whites of her eyes so white. Claire shut her own eyes and breathed, counting, the way she'd learned in Lamaze class.

Then she said, "Don't the courts close early, like banks? It's almost one-thirty. You'd better get going." Confident elder-sister voice, a voice Evvie was used to, which she automatically heeded.

But Evvie said, "Jesus, Claire. Look at it out. I'll go tomorrow, okay?"

The tall windows throbbed with rain. Claire said, "It'll stop soon. It's just a shower. Here." She thrust her fistful of envelopes into Evvie's good hand.

"Tomorrow. Honest. Anyway, I don't have the right clothes. Most of your stuff was too loose. The judge'll think I'm some kind of a flounder." She flicked at her skirt, a rusty black one of Claire's she'd chosen to wear backwards so that the slit exposed one fern-tattooed thigh. "I might as well walk in there packing a bowl, you know?"

Claire felt something give way inside her. "For Christ's sake!" she shouted. "You do it to yourself, Evvie! You smoke dope. You go off your meds—" Oh, it felt good, this anger, never before allowed toward Evvie; it felt glorious. It washed her clean. She rushed on, "You wear the wrong thing, say the wrong thing, you *do* the wrong thing—" Her sister was backing away, holding up her handful of tickets as if to ward off Claire's words. "—and then you expect, you wonder why people, oh, fuck it!"

Evvie stood with her back to the door, staring at her. Astonished. She said plaintively, "I can't. I *can't*. I'm not as strong as you."

"Oh, please. You just don't try. You don't have to. You have me. And Daddy. You're the *youngest*." Claire's voice rose to a whiny parody of her sister's.

"Claire!" Evvie whispered. Her face was white, and the hennaed bangs made a thorny crown across her brow. Her eyes filled with tears. She didn't blink, just let them crawl down her cheeks.

The doorbell rang.

"What!" Claire shouted.

"Smithereens!" sang a cheerful male voice.

Claire reached past Evvie to yank open the door.

A diminutive young man in olive-drab pajamas said, "Smithereens Pest Control! I'm here for those pesky little Stone Age survivors." His smile, as he took in Claire's expression, faltered.

Evvie turned, her cast thumping against the doorframe, and pushed past him. She ran down the hall to the elevator, then stood there, head turned toward Claire, angrily tasting her tears. Her face was no longer imploring; it was furious, determined, utterly reckless.

Foreboding filled Claire. "Evvie!" she called. But she did not leave the doorway. Evvie slapped the elevator button. Its doors parted, and she vanished.

"So . . . where's the problem? Kitchen? Bathroom? They didn't *say* water bugs, but there's a lot of 'em on Fred Street."

The smell of pot roast filled the hallway. She'd never noticed before how much it resembled the smell of shit.

"Ma'am, uh, Miss. Gotta charge you for a house call anyways, so why don't—"

She backed over the threshold and shut the door in the young man's upturned face.

Buried, not cremated. Given whole into the ground, to await the resurrection of the body, in which her father, a Unitarian (her mother had been the Catholic), did not believe. One of the corporal works of mercy, Claire remembered from grade school: to bury the dead. A beautiful, hot, end-of-April morning. Two young boys boxing on the lawn outside the cemetery gates as the limo passed. The minty smell of sun-warmed tar; a family of cardinals in the tulip tree just beginning to shade the new raw grave. Later there would be a headstone, chosen by her father: *God is greater than our hearts and knows all things (1 John 3:20)*. Her mother's stone, on the other side of the tulip tree, said only, "Anna Mullineaux Thrall, February 2, 1939–October 22, 1975." Julia stood across the open grave from Claire, three rosaries wound around her neck with their crosses dropping down between her breasts. Claire stood next to her father; she could smell the sweet old-fashioned stuff he used on his hair, what she and Evvie used to call "hair syrup."

"In the midst of life we are in death," Father Grimaldi said, but made the point (his own) that it could also be the other way round. Claire felt her father's eyes on her then, but she would not look up.

For once the *Sun-Times* had gotten the facts right. A very new driver, a young Hmong woman whose English deserted her, a bus forced to detour because of spring road repair (it was an election year), the top of the bus jammed on the Pidge Avenue overpass. A boy in a rain-soaked red windbreaker. The bus roaring, straining, backward and forward; the boy pacing the aisle, more and more anxious. Finally he pulled a gun out of his backpack, ran to the front of the bus, and put the gun to the driver's head. She fainted. The bus stalled. Evvie, who was sitting near the front, stood up and put her good hand on the boy's shoulder and spoke to him. No one heard what she said, but the middle-aged woman who'd been sitting next to her claimed the boy yelled, "I was born here!" Besides Evelyn Anna Thrall, age twenty-three, two other people were killed, and a six-year-old girl lost the sight of one eye. The boy shot himself through the mouth.

In her father's little house, filled with cellophane-shrouded baskets of fruit, as if someone were going on an ocean voyage, they sat in silence. Nicholas, in his Spider Man shirt and a pair of blue-plaid overalls he was just about to outgrow, crunched Carr's Water Crackers from Vince's towering basket. Watching her father watch her son, Claire thought: To outlive your child has to be the most terrible thing that can happen to you. She thought of the shining coffin with the upper half of its cover thrown back, like a Dutch door; Evvie's skin, against the midnight-blue plush lining, the improbable "flesh" color in Nicholas's box of Crayolas. How clearly *empty* her body was. There was no one in it; Evvie was really gone.

Nicholas, having torn the colored cellophane from all the baskets, began crushing it into bright balls that he flung into the air. They caught the late afternoon sun and sparkled as they fell. When he threw his head back, his thick brown hair (Evvie's hair) gleamed like a bird's wing.

Claire bit into a peach and let its slippery coolness fill her mouth. She had meant to stop sheltering Evvie, to encourage her, brace her. That was what she'd meant to do. Wasn't it?

Why didn't I hold her? Why didn't I let her cry?

Grief is a separate country. Claire, who'd told no one about the fight, found herself isolated, set apart from other people—even from her father—by what she knew. The stark simplicity of cause and effect impaled her. She'd let Evvie—once, *one time* in their whole lives—feel her anger, and Evvie had died. Life was not supposed to work like that. Missed connections, second chances, *the gray area*—without them, how could anyone live? How could you dare to take a single step? For weeks after the funeral she was afraid to leave the loft, afraid to let Nicholas out of her sight. Walking back and forth in bare feet across the bare wood floors, the mail uncollected, the doorbell unanswered. Fear, like a river in winter, embraced her and soaked her through; she had to keep moving or freeze.

Sometimes she'd look down and find an unexpected button or a bit of lace or fringe (many of Evvie's garments had had fringe)—the Hansel-and-Gretel trail Evvie had left everywhere ever since Claire could remember. To lead herself out of the woods? Or to say, I am here; I am lost? And bending down to retrieve a silky scrap, rolling it between her fingers, Claire would feel, for a moment, a small, warm current of relief.

The Ones without Visas ❀

T HEY MET IN SEPTEMBER WHEN ANDREW, WHO TAUGHT MUSIC, was babysitting eighth-grade detention. Julio, written up for cursing in gym, was printing carefully at the bottom of his yellow slip: *Aceto, Julio. A bad word slip out.* Andrew leaned over Julio's shoulder and said, "In Latin your name means 'vinegar.' *Aceto.* Did you know that?" Julio took a handful of Serial Murderers cards out of his back pocket and began to shuffle them. He smelled strongly of tobacco. Andrew leaned closer. "How do you get a nun pregnant?" Julio's eyes slid upward. Andrew whispered, "You tell the priest she's an altar boy." Julio's laughter exploded through his nose; he yanked his T-shirt up over his face and sneezed into it.

That was the year Andrew Rogacz became known throughout Shadyside Middle School as the man who'd turned Julio Aceto around. Because he taught music—a non-academic, non-essential subject— Andrew had grown used to being marginal. The sudden acceptance by his colleagues after six years of invisibility might once have been welcome. But that year Andrew could think of nothing but his baby daughter, Grace—his first child, long awaited, who had been born in August. The other teachers, even the redoubtable Ernest—who sweated profusely, winter and summer, and used expressions like "compassion fatigue"—mistook Andrew's indifference for insight. How else explain his success when everyone else had long since given up? Thirteen-year-old Julio had stolen his first car in sixth grade; had thrown a wastebasket through a window in Mrs. Yerkes's seventh-grade remedial math class; had, in that same class, set fire to the long dark hair of Mee-Na Kim, who sat in front of him. For these and other offenses Julio could never receive worse than three days' suspension, because he was classified as Behaviorally Disturbed.

By Halloween Julio was keeping a journal that he left every Friday, without comment, in Andrew's box in the mailroom. *I think my strenth cold be the idea I put words to. The weeknes is my spellin mos of the time.* Andrew should have been moved by the boy's openness, his trust, but he was not. Nothing moved him except Grace. *Las nite my dad he try to choke my mom with the cord of her curlin iren. I feel life have gon out a shape.* Grace, who by January—her five-month birthday—had never once smiled at him, was not babbling even the most cryptic baby syllables. *There is this girl she look good to me. Yesterday she pass by + I spoke Began to speke.*

Sitting in faculty meetings beside Ernest, who fanned himself with a painted paper fan, Andrew wore his new fame poorly. It was only at these meetings that he felt close to his students. Restlessness combined with torpor and anger at his own helplessness, sitting quiescent among the smells of pencil shavings and oranges and wet wool. It wasn't that he understood his students' feelings, but that he *felt* them. "They come—they go," Ernest said, misunderstanding the cause of Andrew's preoccupation. A hand settled on Andrew's shoulder. "The ones without visas. You know that, buddy."

My girl her name is Ariela, she is new. She teach me dick dissiplin + to love. ARIELA!!! In March the doctors began to test Grace for rare diseases: rogue chromosomes, unnamed viruses, the illness that afflicted King George III. *Her girlfren they are jeallos to her but she say it no mater, what mater is love.* More days than not, Andrew came home from school to find his wife folding laundry—the same tiny garments, over and over—tears rolling unheeded into the hollows of her collarbone. When Grace caught sight of her father, she stretched her arms wide and swiveled her hands like a safecracker, but she did not smile. *Some thing are right wile other are wrong. When I look back at myself now I see I was reall bad. Ariela she help me to see.*

Waiting outside the building for the school bus one April afternoon, Ariela Jimenez was attacked by another seventh-grade girl and the girl's older sister, who cut over fifty percent of her body with a box-cutter. Grace needed new and better doctors, far away in Minnesota, and Andrew took Compassionate Leave. When he returned at the end of May, his daughter having become the property of no-longer-baffled specialists, Julio was gone. In the pile of mail that had accumulated during his absence, Andrew found a battered manila envelope with his name misspelled in large pencilled capitals across the front. *At the hospitle no body tell me wear she is or how. All day I wait heart in mouth but no + no.*

Street of Swans ❀

OCTOBER 1986: ONE MONTH AFTER MY FOUR-YEAR-OLD DAUGHTER, Lucy, and I arrived in Moscow. I spent the morning in our room working on Marina Tsvetayeva, whose poetry I was translating for a small American publisher; then I made the long bus/Metro/trolley trip across Moscow to the embassy. The afternoon was cold and bright, with snow clouds massing above the Lenin Hills. Snow in October! I thought. The trolley wheels sang on the track in Tsvetayeva's spangled, impossible phrases. *You to women like a goblet. A handkerchief at the hour of recklessness.*

The Tuesday mail from Helsinki was in. It was too soon for another letter from Pop, but I went hopefully to the SenEx exchangees' box anyway. What I found was a long brown envelope from the State of Rhode Island, addressed to me in Providence and forwarded to Moscow. Inside was a legal-sized sheet headed "Motion for Clarification." It set the day—yesterday—and time for a hearing in Superior Court concerning the "custody and control of the minor Lucy Ellen Willauer." The plaintiff was Clement Quay; the defendant was me. My hands holding Clement's letter shook so hard the paper made a sound like popcorn popping. I tore the heavy paper across and threw the pieces into the mailroom wastebasket.

In the underground tunnel beneath Tchaikovsky Street—I was

crossing to the trolley stop on my way to pick up Lucy—a tall, thin figure suddenly loomed in front of me. He was shaved bald, bareheaded
despite the dank, bone-deep chill of the tunnel. His careful Russian
was too easy to understand. Where was the Swedish Embassy? South,
along the river, I told him curtly, and started to pass by. He laid an
ungloved hand on my arm. My heart wadded up. He stood there,
silent; his grip tightened. Then two middle-aged women, arm in arm,
came trundling toward us. The man's grip loosened slightly. I shook
myself free and ran up the steps to the street.

My trolley had gone. I turned to see the man emerging onto the
sidewalk behind me. My heart was beating so heavily I could feel it.
Crossing the trolley tracks—strictly forbidden—I began to run in the
opposite direction, down Tchaikovsky Street towards the Arbat.

People stared at me, a tall woman running, flag of long, loose
hair as obviously foreign as my puffy yellow parka. I felt their glances
without really noticing them, like the snowflakes sifting down from the
cloud-clogged sky. The string bag of dirty clothes—I'd been so upset I'd
forgotten to drop it off at the embassy's laundry—thudded against my
legs. I ran along Tchaikovsky Street—not the shortest way to Lucy, but
the way I knew—across the Arbat to crowded Smolensky Boulevard.
Was he still behind me? I couldn't stop to turn around. Worming coins
out of the inside pocket of my parka, wrong size, flinging them away to
grab a fresh fistful. Coins ringing on the cobblestones, people's astonished faces. Snow falling more thickly now. My chest ached. Sweat
iced my face and neck.

There, finally—*there*, on the corner of Leninsky Prospekt—the
heartening vermilion of the No. 33 trolley that went down Vavilova to
Lucy's Soviet preschool. I grabbed the hand that stretched out to me
as the trolley pulled away and was hauled up onto the steps. When I
turned around, the man was gone.

Could Clement have sent him?

Stomach still scurrying with fear, I hung onto an overhead strap, wedged upright by the bodies all around me. The oniony smell of my own sweat blended with the usual warm cloud of body odors. I comforted myself with lesser dangers. The KGB. A small-time thug from Zagorsk trolling for dollars.

I'd moved out when I was six months pregnant, when a last, terrible, wounding fight had made it clear no baby was going to change Clement. I was thirty-one, old enough to know better. Clement, who was forty-five and had a grown son in Seattle, had made it clear from the start he wanted no more children. (He hadn't wanted to marry again, either, but he'd been afraid—back then—of losing me.) His son Joshua was enough, Clement said, when I tried to persuade him; with Joshua, Clement's line—as he put it—would continue. Suppose Joshua didn't marry or have children? I'd ask. But Clement refused to consider that possibility.

I delivered my baby with Pop as my labor coach. Clement didn't acknowledge my note about Lucy's birth; he didn't try to see her. I told myself it was for the best, that it would help me get over him, and eventually I did get over him, the only way anyone ever does. I fell in love with someone new. There's an old Russian saying: *The only true love affair is the one between mother and child.* Gradually Lucy made me all one piece again; I got used to living without pain; I almost got used to being happy.

The divorce came through when Lucy was two and a half; Clement, who'd stayed in New York while I went back to Providence, didn't contest it. He didn't come to the final hearing. Then, last August, just after Lucy's fourth birthday, came that first formal letter suggesting that we meet "to consider the child's future." In an instant I saw the legal case

Clement could make. He was a high-powered, highly paid economist, a respected academic, an advisor to the government. And what was I? A single mother, self-employed, child in day care, tiny apartment in a questionable city neighborhood. Rationality deserted me. This is my punishment, I thought, remembering how the needle had trembled in my fingers when I'd poked the holes in my diaphragm. This is my punishment for making Clement a father against his will.

That night, though, when I told Pop, he said, Why now? Why, after more than four years, would Clement suddenly want a child he'd never even seen? He did a little sleuthing, my brilliant uneducated father, and found out why. Clement's son, Joshua, had been killed by a hit-and-run driver the month before.

A few days later I saw the announcement in *Translators' Quarterly* of a last-minute vacancy on the SenEx exchange for the fall semester. The USSR had seemed safe, the Iron Curtain an impenetrable shield between Clement and Lucy. Between Clement and me.

"That's really all I can do? Now, if you were Foreign Service?" Roberta Reeder's sentences turned up at the end, ingratiatingly; hers was a professional regret polished by years of bureaucratic abrasion. Somewhere along the way she seemed to have mislaid her eyebrows. The penciled replacements rose in feathery faux concern.

Lucy sat on the thick plum carpet with a copy of *Amerika!*, the state department's Russian-language propaganda magazine, turning over pages full of glossy smiles. She was being too good; it couldn't last.

I leaned forward, my elbows toppling two of the neat piles of papers on the desk. Roberta Reeder flinched. I said, "Look, Ms. Reeder. I need your help. I'm an American citizen. My daughter is an American citizen. This is our embassy."

"I'm sorry? I know it must seem — unfair." Roberta Reeder's Rhode

Island accent—she would have called my father a "security god"—made it sound like "unfear." "If it were an emergency? A death, or an accident. In the old days . . . But this is 1986. Things are easier now, with *Perestroika* and all? You're a professional translator, Ms. Willauer. Surely your Russian is fluent? You could put in a phone call to the States. You could send a telegram—"

"The earliest I could reserve a phone call for was Tuesday. This is Thursday." I heard my voice getting louder, shriller. Lucy retired behind her magazine, holding it high in not-very-clean hands; OKT'ABR '86! the red-white-and-blue cover cheered. She should have been at preschool, but I'd needed to keep her close.

"I'm sorry." No sweet upward tilt this time. "Embassy communications facilities are solely for the use of Foreign Service personnel."

I restrained an impulse to sweep my arm across the desk and scatter papers to the four corners of the room. In the old, childless days I might very well have done it. But now I couldn't afford to alienate this woman, the Press & Cultural attaché, a fellow New Englander who, up until half an hour ago, had seemed a potential ally.

"All right," I said, rising. I made myself add, "Thank you." I put out a hand to Lucy. "Come on, Goose. Let's go get some lunch."

Lucy clutched the magazine to her chest, crumpling several pages.

"You can take that with you, hon?" Roberta Reeder said. She came around the front of her desk to speed us on our way. I saw from her lips-only smile that I'd made an enemy.

Lucy saw it, too. She shook her head violently. She set the magazine on the radiator and grabbed my hand. Before we were through the outer office of Press & Cultural, where a young Russian secretary sat picking her cuticle, I could hear Roberta Reeder's marmalade voice on the telephone. "About the ambassador's reception tomorrow? Are you sure you have enough cheers?"

I tightened my grip on Lucy's hand and walked with fast, thudding steps down the hall towards the stairs, muttering, "Thanks for nothing. *Nada, nichts, nichevo.* You cow, *Kuh, korova!*"

Lucy said, "She fuckindammit, Mama?"

Two Russians in green overalls were peering down the elevator shaft. A hand-lettered sign taped to the wall said, "NA REMONT/ ON REPAIR. WE REGRET THAT YOU WILL BE UNBEARABLE."

At the top of the stairs I thrust the door open, feeling too late some resistance from the other side. There was a thud and some shuffling, a curse. "*Chort!*"

It was the Russian liaison for the Academy of Sciences exchange. I'd met him at an embassy reception, but I couldn't remember his name.

"Sorry," I muttered.

He took no notice of my sullenness. "It is Gainor Willauer, is it not?" He hunkered down on his haunches next to Lucy. "And who is this?"

"This is my—"

"Lucy Lucechka!" Lucy interrupted. "Lucechka" was the Russian nickname they'd given her at preschool.

"I am Aleksandr Rosanov. Americans call me Rose."

Somewhere someone began hammering on metal, a distant clanging. Eyes on Rosanov's bushy grizzled beard, Lucy shook her head and laughed her throaty laugh.

"No? What do you mean, no?"

"That's a flower! You're not a flower."

"Honest, it is what everybody calls me."

Lucy shook her head again. For a moment she looked heart-stoppingly like Clement: pointed chin, imperious ripe-olive eyes. I thought, Damned if she isn't flirting with him.

"Well . . . Russian persons are calling me Sasha."

Still eye to eye with him, Lucy considered this. "Sosh," she assented.

"*Ostorozhno!*" A green-clad workman came through the door, thrusting our little group into a corner of the landing.

"Better we go down," Rosanov said. He stood up and pressed against the wall to let me go first.

"But you were on your way up."

"Changed my mind."

Out on Tchaikovsky Street I bent to button Lucy's Soviet-made fur coat. I pulled a soft white knitted hat out of my parka pocket and settled it on her head, tying it under her chin. Lucy, absorbed in a pigeon's progress along the curb, forgot to squirm. One-handed, Rosanov buttoned a pea jacket that looked like a relic of the seventies and turned up the collar, then pulled on a dark-blue wool beret. His left hand remained in his pocket as if sewn there.

"Where you are headed?" he asked.

I hadn't thought beyond getting out of the building without inflicting bodily harm on any of the embassy staff.

"*Smotrit'e*, ah, Gainor. You look deeply unhappy on the stairs, when we bump. Is it something I could help?"

At the word "help," I suddenly felt my eyes burn. The No. 10 trolley clanged past, its bright red bleeding onto the gray stones of Tchaikovsky Street. I found myself telling Aleksandr "Rose" Rosanov how one of the *dezhurnayas*—women who sat, day and night, next to the elevator on each floor of the building where the exchangees lived—had knocked on our door that morning while Lucy and I were having our breakfast of black bread with elderberry jam, tea, and Tang. I'd had to shove the forbidden hot plate under the bed in order to accept my father's telegram, sent in answer to my own three days before.

I pulled the crumpled gray paper out of the inner pocket of my parka and smoothed it out for Rosanov to see.

CEMENT A WAY STOP LET HER FLOW STOP LOV POP.

That morning the incomprehensibility of this had undone me. I'd sat on the bed crying onto a velveteen rabbit and a one-armed panda, piled into my lap by Lucy, until the smell of heated iron from the bedsprings made me remember the hot plate.

"I don't know what to do," I finished. The phone call booked for days away, the embassy unwilling to help. All my translator's empathy had failed to decode Pop's telegram. Clement away—on way?—letter follows. Away, or on the way? It was crucial to know which. I leaned against the yellow stucco wall of the embassy. A cold breeze glued strands of my ponytail across my mouth.

Rosanov said, "You have send your telegram by means of telephone?"

I nodded. Lucy, tired of pigeons, came and tugged at the hem of my parka.

Why not try again, in person, Rosanov urged; the International Telegraph Office was just over on Gorky Street, we could take a taxi. "Bored bored *bored* bored bored," Lucy chanted, swinging in circles around my legs. And afterward we could go to the little park near Novodevichy Convent and see the swans.

"Swans!" cried Lucy. She threw herself against my knees and squeezed till they buckled.

The golden domes of Novodevichy shone against a cold bright sky. Its walls of dusty, pale stone—once a prison for troublesome ladies of noble birth—made me think of sugar cookies. We sat, Rose (it was Rose now) and I, on a bench in the little park that bordered the convent's south wall. Noon sun warmed our faces. Lucy stood at the edge of the pond, her feet planted among tall, frost-stiffened grasses.

"We have luck," Rose said. "This might be the last day before the lake freezes over. What they do with the swans then, I do not know."

A widening band of cloudy ice crept toward the center of the pond. The swans stayed farther out, ignoring the crusts thrown by *babushkas* and cheeky babies. They dipped their beaks to their own reflections or swam in semi-circles, lifting their black-masked heads like glamorous bandits. I tried unsuccessfully to resist the trail of thought that led from swans to birds to Clement, who was (in his own phrase) a world-class ornithologist.

It felt good to have sent the telegram. A message even now on its way, traveling through its own mysterious dimension, to Pop. "Let me talk," Rose had said when our taxi pulled up outside the yellow stucco palace on Gorky Street. Inside, we stood under an enormous red poster: "LENIN LIVED, LENIN LIVES, LENIN SHALL LIVE." A young woman in a hairnet whose English was nearly flawless emerged from the nether regions of the Mezhdunarodny Telegraf, and I saw my words faithfully set down on lined yellow paper. Who knew what had been made of the earlier telegram? *Traduttore, traditore.* I'd quoted the old saying to Rose: *to translate is to betray.*

Rose stretched out his feet in puffy brown Soviet shoes, as if the sun might reach through to the toes inside. His ungloved hands lay in his lap, the left one—deformed in some way I couldn't quite see—underneath the right. He turned up his face to the sun and shut his eyes. Up close he wasn't as young as he'd seemed.

I kept my eyes on Lucy, though there wasn't much chance she'd wander off. Lucy loved swans, had always loved them (her father's blood?); every evening she made me mistranslate our bus stop, Ulitsa

Lebedeva—sung out by the conductor on the way home from pre-school—as Street of Swans, though Swanson Street would have been more accurate. There was hardly anybody in the park—a few old people accompanied by small children, one or two men strolling with open coats. Any of them could have been low-level KGB assigned to follow American exchangees. Even that black-coated *babushka* with the shawl over her head, walking along the gravel path to the pond. Or not. They don't have to follow you all the time; they only have to make you think they do.

The air held the astringent, cindery smell of approaching snow. Our silence on the sunny bench was not uncomfortable, but it wasn't relaxed, either. We sat with shoulders just not touching. Rose leaned forward, refolded his hands (Look? Don't look?), shifted his legs. The small motions communicated themselves as a sort of trilling in my own body. Was it only me? Because it had been so long since Clement?

At the water's edge the old woman in the iris-printed shawl stopped next to Lucy. She patted her bulging black cloth bag and said some-thing, leaning down. I half-stood—not even that, but Rose felt the movement. He laid a hand on my arm. "It is all right," he said. "See? She is giving only some bread, for the swans."

I relaxed, but not all the way. Lucy's arm went up; a dark crescent arced and fell short of two indifferent swans. Lucy looked back at us and laughed. Rose took his hand away. In the sunlight his eyes were the red-brown of the cardamom seeds Clement used to put in curry. They regarded me with a combination of sympathy and lust. Embarrassed at the pleasure this gave me, I looked past Rose at the shining domes of Novodevichy, their shape more like turnips than onions, piercing the black grid of electricity cables and telephone wires like a glimpse of gold teeth in the mouths of *babushkas*.

"Who is this Clement?" Rose asked abruptly. "Is he your hus-band?"

His voice said he'd been there, on the other side of marriage, where a child is no longer something miraculous you made together, but something to be disputed. I kept my eyes on Lucy's cherry-red back as I spoke. "Ex-husband." A slump, a slight exhalation of relief from the body beside mine? "He's Lucy's father."

In the middle of the pond a swan rose up, arched, and shook its chest feathers furiously. A shout came from its beak. Lucy laughed up at her attendant *babushka*.

"I think he wants to take her away from me."

Then I found myself telling Rose everything. How I'd left Clement before Lucy was born and hadn't seen him since, how he'd never even seen Lucy ("*Chort!*" Rose muttered). About the death of Clement's son and the letter from him in August that had sent me here, to Moscow. I left out the fact that I'd tricked Clement into fatherhood.

Rose said, "I was born in Kiev. Diplom, Moscow State University, 1963. Failed Medical School. Sent to New York, USA, 1965 to 1967, to train in medical photography. Married, 1968, one child"—he paused, looking happy and sad at the same time—"Kolya, born 1972. Widowed, 1974. Married, 1983; divorced in July. Now I am . . . *odinokii*. How is it said?"

"Unattached. You were married twice?"

"I like to be married. To be . . . attached." He sighed, a shoes-up Russian sigh. "*Nado umet' xotet*. Do you know this proverb? One can have what one wants in life. But only if one knows how to want."

So Rose had a son. Born in 1972—that would make him fourteen. Something told me not to ask more, at least not now.

There was a sudden wild commotion among the swans. Someone must have thrown them something desirable, shattering their sangfroid. "*Shto takoye!* Look at that!" the *babushka's* cry drifted back to us, followed by Lucy's enthusiastic echo, "Shit takoy!"

Watching her stand on tiptoe to throw a crust, Rose said in Russian, as if to himself, "You must love them too much. Must. Otherwise, how can you give them all they need from you?"

I thought of how Tsvetayeva's daughter had died of starvation in the great Moscow famine during the winter of 1920. She would have been about three then—only a year younger than Lucy. They were offered refuge in France, but Tsvetayeva refused to leave her country. What would she have thought, I wondered, of the Russian women who married American men to escape from the Soviet Union, women who offered themselves in catalogues, brides of men they'd never met?

What would she have thought of me?

Lucy chattered all the way to the bus stop. "*Babushkas* know a lot. They're not just grown-up—they're *past* grown-up. We don't have a *babushka or* a dad. But we have a grandpa. Look—a *byelka*! Swans are *lebedi*. Mama, why don't fishes drowned?"

At the corner of Pirogovsky Street there was the usual clutch of dark-coated, fur-hatted Russians, but not in the usual orderly queue. They were clustered around something. Lucy let Rose lift her up onto his shoulders. We pushed our way in until we could see a man standing beside a board displaying Halloween masks. They were rubber, cleverly painted and lifelike. Gorbachev, a gorilla, Nixon, a white-haired woman I didn't recognize. The man hawking them wore the face of Stalin.

"Down!" Lucy cried, frightened. We extricated ourselves from the crowd and Rose lowered her gently to the sidewalk.

"We *always* have lunch now," Lucy whined. "I'm hungry, Mama. You're starving me crazy."

The No. 64 bus pulled up. With a single motion everyone around us turned away from the masks. I picked up Lucy. There were cries of *Mat' s rebyonkom*! "Mother with child!" The crowd parted; hands thrust out to push us along to the front of the line. Lucy threw Rose a ravishing glance and cried, "Bye-bye, Sosh!"

"Wait! When shall we meet again? Gainor!"

I couldn't see him through the crush of bodies sweeping me up onto the steps of the bus. It was all I could do to keep my footing, keep Lucy's and my combined weight steady. I tried to turn around, but I couldn't. There were no phone books in the Soviet Union, no listings of private citizens' numbers anywhere. I threw back my head and shouted numbers into the bright sky. "*Dva! Dva! Vosem'! Shest'! Shest'! Dva! Tri!*" Tongues clicked at this (but then, a foreigner, *Ameri-kanka*, what could one expect?), and those near my end of the queue risked their places to crane and stare.

Lucy's arm tightened around my neck. We were swept upward into the bus. I tried to see Rose, but there were too many people between me and the windows. Had he heard me? Unaccountably, the idea that I might not see him again made me sad.

"Mama!" Lucy said into my ear. "I have to pee."

How much do you really know about this guy? Pop would have demanded. A divorced medical photographer from Kiev, in his (maybe) mid-forties. He'd lived in the West, went freely to the embassy—either he had friends in high places, or he was KGB. Diabolical of him to offer Lucy swans. How did he know? Oh, of course: his own child. (Custody problems? Worse?) What had made me tell him so much?

Until the moments in the Mezhdunarodny Telegraf with Rose beside me, I had not truly understood how alone I was. I thought of those lyre-necked swans, so graceful and imperious and calm, while beneath the water line their feet shuttled furiously.

. . . .

> TELEFON IMPOSSIBLE STOP WAIT FOUR LETTER STOP
> ALL LOV POPP

Lucy sat on the floor just outside the circle of light from my desk lamp, carefully prying apart the halves of a *matryoshka* doll, while I read Pop's letter. She was good with her hands; she'd inherited her grandfather's dexterity. "Ho!" she exclaimed, in pure but theatrical joy, each time a painted wooden head came off.

Clement was here with some guy in a three-piece suit & asked a lot of questions. Are you with Lucy all day, do you ever leave her alone in the apartment, etc.

"Look, Mama!" cried Lucy. "Mama, look!"

Six wooden dolls (this *matryoshka* was the deluxe model) marched across the polished parquet floor, top halves in one row, bottoms in the other. Each row was lined up in meticulously graduated order, except for the last, smallest doll, which stood whole and alone.

"Very nice, Goose," I said.

Three-Piece Suit asked the questions. Peter Pan just stood there with his Environmental Expression. I did a little lawyering of my own & found out, they can't make the Russians send you back for this kind of thing. Murder, maybe; but not custody. So you & the Goose are okay. for now. Think rationally! Can you manage to stay on there? Anything you want me to do on this end, just say. Give my Lucy Goose a big hug and 100+ kisses.

Lucy began putting the dolls back together one by one. Outside the door to our room an old-fashioned carpet sweeper trundled back and forth with a gravelly sound. I reread Pop's letter for the fifth or sixth time, as if I could wear it down, smooth it into old news; finally, defeated, I folded it back into its envelope. For Clement to come to Pop—that seemed ominous. I knew how tenacious Clement could be when he wanted something: once, for a time, I had been that something.

If only I could see Pop, get the details. If I could just have him *here*. His Humphrey Bogart voice, his smell of Fels Naphtha soap and machine oil. Since my mother left, when I was four, Pop had never not been there. Pop had been my Lamaze partner, had told me bracing, apocryphal stories of women who delivered their babies themselves, severing the umbilical cord with their teeth, had coached me through Lucy's birth. Pop was the only person alive who knew I'd tricked Clement into fatherhood.

I stuffed the letter inside my Müller-Smirnitsky dictionary. "Come on, Goose. Time for bed."

"Ho!" cried Lucy, joining together the last doll.

"Come on, let's find your pj's."

"Mama. It's not time yet."

"It's seven-thirty," I lied. "What story do you want tonight?"

"No story! It is *not* time!"

It took all my strength to haul a protesting Lucy onto her bed in the corner, pull pajama bottoms up over locked knees. She was acting up in response to my own tenseness—the mother part of me knew that. The rest of me said, Tapped out, and wished I were nobody's mother. At last I handed Lucy Sobachka, the earless, indeterminate stuffed animal (only its name indicated doghood) she'd smuggled home from preschool during her first week there. The creature's worn beige fur was like a bathrobe of my mother's, remembered only as a smell, a texture; one black shoe-button eye was loose, giving it a wry, knowing expression. Lucy looked up and said, "I want Tanna. Tanna is *nice*."

Tatiana Stefanovna was her preschool teacher. I kissed my daughter's wide, warm forehead, then drew the curtain around her bed. Behind it she began to sob, a dry, hopeless, unchildlike sound.

Backing away, I stepped into the row of dolls. They scattered like tiny bowling pins, clicking hollowly, wood against wood, over the parquet floor.

"Mama!"

"Shh. It's okay. Go to sleep now."

Turning off the lamp, I heard Lucy begin, hiccupping sleepily, to comfort herself. "*Sobachka, sobachka*," she whispered. "*Byelka, byelka, byelka.*" Little dog, little squirrel. I sat down on the floor and picked up the nearest—the tiniest—doll. Think rationally, I told myself, in Pop's voice. Okay—Clement couldn't get Lucy out of the USSR legally. He might, just might, have sent the guy in the tunnel, as some kind of warning. He might even come to Moscow himself—he probably knew some politician who could get him a visa. My grip on the little doll tightened. The doll spurted out of my grasp, bounced twice, and rolled out of sight.

I stood looking out into the moonless night, the darkness grasping at the blue glow of the BALATON sign across the street. Quiet, so quiet for a city, the street empty except for a few buses and taxis and the occasional owl-eyed black government car.

Think rationally. Clement wouldn't risk doing anything illegal. That would jeopardize his career, the thing he cared for most. As long as we stayed here, Lucy and I were safe. But my SenEx visa expired at New Year's. Nine weeks from now. Tourist visas for the Soviet Union took months to process, and were often refused. So that was out. I would have to throw myself on the mercy of the Foreign Service. Get them to take me on as a secretary, a cleaning lady, anything. Tomorrow—I'd go to the embassy tomorrow.

Lucy would miss her doll in the morning. Wearily I crawled under the desk and shoved my hand into the dust-furred underpinnings of the radiator. The thin wood had cracked. I could feel a jagged fissure running from the gentle swell of its belly to the top of its head. The broken edge bit into my thumb. I backed slowly out from under the desk and stood in the blue-washed darkness holding onto the doll, as if the pressure of my palm could anneal it.

On the first of November I found a sealed envelope, thick and cream-colored and crested, in my mailbox at the embassy. Roberta Reeder regretted there was no possibility of extending my SenEx visa. I ran upstairs to Press & Cultural to plead with her, but she was in Helsinki getting her hair done. I sat on the floor outside the ambassador's office and refused to leave until he saw me. But it was no good. We had until New Year's, when my SenEx appointment ended.

Back in our room, in despair, I thought wistfully of Rose's ready sympathy, his odd combination of calm practicality and a romantic heart. He had phoned three times in the two weeks since Novodevichy—he'd been sent unexpectedly to Kiev—but the probability of government eavesdroppers had killed my urge to confide in him.

Was it then the idea first came to me? Russian women married in order to leave; I needed to stay. Marriage could make that possible, too.

He was waiting for me outside the Zenith Cinema. When the trolley door folded back, his upturned face, its curly surround of beard and hair glinting in the snow-flocked light from the street lamp, gave me a start of pleasure. That look of expectancy—expecting *me*. I remembered the sense of safety I'd felt standing beside him in the Mezhdunarodny Telegraf three weeks before. The corset of unease I seemed to wear all the time loosened, and I breathed in great gulps of the cold sharp air.

We went straight in—Rose had already bought tickets—and fumbled our way into seats in the dark. The film, in rickety, rushing black and white, had already started. *October: Ten Days That Shook the World.* Grim faces under karakul hats, row upon row of bayonets and scythes, women in blankets waiting wearily for bread. It was a silent film, with titles. "THIS IS THE MINISTER OF WAR. WHERE ARE THE COSSACKS?" Over Shostakovich's music, incessant and sour-sounding, Rose said, in Russian, "For this film Eisenstein had eight thousand extras. Many played themselves; they were actually present in 1917." The dusty, camphor-smelling darkness filled with vigorous shushing. We watched several matrons in flower-laden hats club two young revolutionaries to death with their parasols.

I was aware of Rose next to me, his size, his awkwardness. Like a boy, he couldn't seem to sit still: he rocked, leaned forward, worked his hands, shifted his legs. From time to time our shoulders touched, a brief sparkling. All of this seemed to go on without me, as if our two bodies were having a separate colloquy of their own. "THE WOMEN'S DEATH BATTALION." Rose smelled of plain, harsh Soviet soap that reminded me of Fels Naphtha. "TO THE LAST DROP OF BLOOD!"

At the interval the lights came up, and we followed the crowd into the lobby. Its marble expanse, smelling of wet wool and sunflower oil, discouraged small talk. The Russians around us, their cigarettes swirling smoke, discussed the film with a carping admiration. Rose's restless body and Eisenstein's images had driven out all thoughts of Clement; now I began to worry again. Almost a week since the embassy had denied my visa extension, and I'd done nothing. Beside me Rose seemed shy, short of words, as if our brief, stilted telephone conversations while he was in Kiev had somehow erased Novodevichy. We stopped beside a vaguely classical white plaster torso, armless and legless, on a black marble pedestal.

"It is a demi-god," said Rose. Most ordinary citizens would have been afraid to speak English in a crowd of other Russians, but then, as I'd begun to see that afternoon at Novodevichy, Rose was no ordinary citizen. Next to the influence someone like Rose could have, Clement's connections would amount to about as much as a sewing circle.

"Demi-god," Rose said again.

"How do you know?"

"Because half of him is missing."

I laughed out loud. The spice-brown eyes regarded me with a pleased expression. I felt myself blushing, and saw that he was, too. Awkwardly, like a couple of teenagers, the two of us stood regarding the plaster demi-god in silence.

Then Rose said, "Gainor. You would like to leave?"

Lucy was safe in the care of the *dezhurnaya*. I'd left them, flushed and laughing, leapfrogging down the hall in a wild game of *Pryg-Skok*. "We'll miss the storming of the Winter Palace," I said.

"We know how it turns out."

I watched him cross the lobby to the vestibule where two old women, knitting fiercely, watched over rows of meek winter coats. Lights blinked curtly in their sconces, signaling the end of the interval. Rose didn't drop the collar of my coat onto my neck as if it burned him, the way most men did. I felt his fingers graze my nape.

There was a dead mouse lying in the middle of the stairs. "Maybe it dies of Shostakovich," Rose said. Laughing, we leaped over it and ran, two truants, down the last steps and out into the dark. When our feet struck the snowy sidewalk, I skidded. I grabbed for Rose's arm, then stopped.

"You can hold to me," he said. He pulled my gloved hand through the crook of his arm and held it there. The cold, clear air was like spirits

of ammonia after the smoke-filled lobby. Our boots squeaked cheerfully on the packed snow.

In the Moscow Metro, built deep to double as a bomb shelter,
the escalators are terrifyingly steep and fast. I stepped on behind Rose,
keeping one hand on the railing. Below us a fur-hatted couple rode
facing each other, the man on the lower step with his back to the
void. They looked as if they'd spent the evening riding up and down.
This might well be the only place they could go to be together, bodies touching, belly to belly, in their heavy coats. The graveyard smell
of damp earth and stone made me shiver. Rose turned around and
stepped up to the step below mine. Face to face now, so close I could
see the gleam of scalp through his curly grizzled hair, could smell its
nutlike odor. "Gloves, they are *prezervativi* — condoms — for hands," he
said. He worked off my right glove, finger by finger. His hand was cold.
We rode, palms touching, past a dizzying succession of amber lights on
poles. I felt the escalator's sinking like desire.

If Rose's studio had had a balcony, it would have been possible, by
craning upward, to glimpse the giant red star on top of the Kremlin.
I unwound my hair and shook it, and drops of melted snow flew off
and ticked against the window glass. Looking down, I watched two
women in headscarves and padded coats move snow from one part of
the sidewalk to another. I could hear, through the cold glass, the rhythmic ring of their shovels. A lullaby. I thought of Lucy, asleep by now
under the watchful gaze of the *dezhurnaya*. Safe. I must have been the
only Westerner in the Soviet Union that night who regarded the Iron
Curtain with affection.

Rose's happiness disclosed itself like a fragrance radiating from
him when he moved. He hung our coats in the huge painted ward-
robe. He brought me commissary brandy in a painted wooden cup.

Then he went over to the varnished yellow cabinets that lined one wall of the big room, opened a door, and fiddled with something. A brief, ugly scraping sound ("*Chort!*" shouted Rose), and then a tenor voice, singing.

"Roland Hayes." Rose stood awkwardly next to me. We watched a cloud overtake the moon, moving as if it had a destination. He downed his brandy in one long fervent swallow. "A very old recording. He was American, the first black man I ever saw. Papa took me to hear him sing, in Helsinki. I was then perhaps seven or eight years old."

Bist du bei mir, geh' ich mit Freude. The voice lifted, iridescent with loneliness, and soared easily above the suave constraining beat of the organ.

I translated softly, "If you are with me, I will go gladly," then saw that Rose didn't need me to. I set my untouched cup on the windowsill. His hands rested on the sill; his eyes were closed. He seemed to have forgotten me, forgotten everything but the music. Yellow light from the lamp behind us shone on his two stumps ("'Member Sosh has those little, *simple* fingers?" Lucy'd said when I kissed her goodbye), the shiny mottled skin stretched tight. They did not look incomplete, but finished in their own way.

I turned and wandered around the sparsely furnished room, anonymous enough to disguise anything, skirting the quilt-covered bed that both of us had carefully avoided looking at. There was a pair of shoes in the bookcase, two mismatched gloves among the drifts of paper on the desk. I had the impression only a resolute lack of possessions stood between Rose and chaos. The photographs taped to the gray-painted walls said his mind was elsewhere.

Roland Hayes sang, *Es drückten deine schone Hände mir die getreuen Augen zu.* Your beautiful hands my faithful eyes would close.

Rose came up behind me, skidding a little on the waxed linoleum.

I was looking at what seemed to be a photograph of the surface of the moon.

"Taken with a fiber-optic probe," he said. "New technique, still experimental."

"Where is it?"

"Inside an old man's knee. See? Light is traveling down fibers to a tiny camera at end."

He followed me along the wall. There were two photographs of a woman's torso with a dark grin where the left breast would have been. A series of naked children—no, it was the same child over and over—walking on all fours like a dog, advancing, with each frame, a small distance forward. ("Gait studies," said Rose, "poorly healed fibular fracture.") A close-up of a single eye, the iris a brilliant lighted jigsaw. A statue toppled onto its back, rough-carved and painted some dark color. Rose lingered by this last one.

"In August I gave *kratkii kurs*—workshop?—on burn photography at the No. 6 clinic. On Shchukinskaya Street. They bring there the survivors from Chernobyl."

"You mean—" I stopped, horrified. It was human?

"This, he is Slava Brazhnik. I liked him—he laughed at my jokes. Not laughed, exactly. *Drozhal* . . . shimmered?"

"Shivered."

"Shivered, all over his body. He died in September."

Not only was it human; it was, had been, alive. I saw, now, the lashless eyes in the charred face. Lustrous white stones.

Rose felt my shudder. He put his hands on my shoulders and turned me around.

"Ah," he said gently. "I am sorry. You see, never anyone comes here, I forget how these things . . . It is what I do, that is all. It is what I can do. I cannot take away their pain, I cannot even understand it, but I can record. Gainor. I am sorry."

His happiness had gone, as if switched off. I wanted it back. I wanted it for myself as much as for him, wanted the safety of that happiness. And it rested—already I understood this about Rose—on his believing he made *me* happy.

I took his hands from my shoulders and held them. My fingers folded over the two stumps, like warm polished thimbles. The way Rose looked at me then told me that, if I chose, we could be safe for always, Lucy and me. We could stay in Russia.

There was just time enough to hope what I felt now wasn't, would never be, love. Love was what I'd had with Clement, and I did not want that, ever again. Over Rose's shoulder I could see the wide bed, its deep-blue quilt a lake of promise in the lamplight. I led him away from the dog-child, the man made of cinders. Away from whatever pain of his own (his face in the park at Novodevichy, his wistfulness with Lucy) these photographs obliquely cherished.

The record ended; the needle lifted and clicked into its cradle. In the silence came the chime of snow shovels, like far-off bells. Rose kissed the way he drank brandy. After that I did not need to do any more.

Iggy Ugly ❁

HALF A RAINBOW CLIMBED THE LATE AFTERNOON SKY, ITS COLORS slowly emerging—first red and orange, then bitter yellow, then green, blue, indigo, and violet—to puzzle Andrew Rogacz. The way it broke off just before the arc began to turn. He braced for a pelting of unanswerable meteorological questions from Iggy, then, looking down, saw she was asleep. Her legs were tucked up so that her whole body (small for a six-year-old) fit into the old Porsche's bucket seat; her face was wedged against the window. Andrew watched the moist cloud of her breath come and go on the glass. From this angle she looked normal, like any ordinary unhappy child.

The bray of a truck horn yanked his eyes back to the road. But he was already, instinctively, swerving to the right. The tachometer shot past the red line. The Porsche, old as it was, responded. The semi splashed by in a roar of spray, with inches to spare.

Andrew fought the chattering in his skull that he refused to call fear, and slowly eased up on the accelerator. On an impulse, he swung off at the next exit. They were on their way home to Pittsburgh from Boston, and he'd planned to stop for the night in Scranton, the halfway point. But it was late: the neurosurgeons at Mass General had taken much longer than he'd expected to evaluate (their ugly word) his daughter. And Providence's meager skyline seemed to beckon. They might as well stop here.

Half a fucking rainbow, for Christ's sake.

"Let. Go. And. Let. Let—" Iggy read the motel clerk's T-shirt out loud.

"Guys," Andrew supplied automatically.

The clerk, a very young woman with a curly side-slung ponytail and a rose tattooed on one cheek, said without looking up, "Cad?"

Probably he was, Andrew thought. Or at least a jerk (Clio's favorite word for him lately). But how would this girl, barely older than his middle-school students, know that? "Sorry," he said. "What did you say?"

"Visa or Mastacad?"

"Cash." His credit cards were maxed out, as usual.

There was a tiny portable TV on the counter, and the clerk kept her eyes on it while her hands busied themselves with his money.

"Let go and let guys," Iggy repeated happily. She liked to reread a sentence whole and smooth, once she'd sounded out its parts. It reminded him of Clio, the way she'd print a photograph over and over until it satisfied her. Iggy had read aloud every billboard, road sign, T-shirt, and legible bit of graffiti they'd encountered since leaving Pittsburgh three days before. She never asked what any of it meant (a fortunate thing, in view of some of the graffiti); the pure act of deciphering was enough for her. Andrew hadn't realized until this trip how the world badgered the literate.

The clerk held out a key and said, "Two-twenty-six, around the back and—" She looked up for the first time and saw Iggy.

Andrew, who'd neglected to brace himself as he usually did, felt the quick itch of anger, felt his face grow hot. He was the only man he knew who still blushed.

As he opened his mouth to crush her with one of his prepared responses, the girl (no prize in the looks department herself) recovered. "up the center stairs," she finished, staring down at Iggy, whose small, sad-grumpy face did not change. Her root beer-colored eyes—her one lovely feature—regarded the clerk with what only Andrew could recognize as hope.

Coaxingly the clerk said, "There's an indoor pool downstairs. It's open till eight. It's wicked nice."

Then, as Iggy failed to return her smile, the clerk shrugged. "Swim at your own risk," she said to Andrew, and thrust the key at him.

The old frustration seized him—*Do* something, jerk—though he knew it was useless. He took the key and turned away without thanks, erasing the girl as he'd taught himself to do. She was nothing—less than nothing. She was what the boys in his seventh-grade music class would have called dick-puke.

Swimming, his daughter was beautiful. She was Grace then—her real name—"Iggy" cast aside like a skin worn only on land. Her face shone as her head turned, rhythmically, towards Andrew and then away. Her body shone: hard-working legs, opal gleam of elbows, flash of a cupped hand. The water, charged with her motion, accepted her over and over. The smell of chlorine, the water's light slap against his daughter's skin, reached Andrew like a telegram from happier times. Watching, he felt his anger slide away into the echoing air.

GIRL, 5, CHOKES TO DEATH ON SLIDE
BOWLING BALL STRIKES 8-MONTH-OLD IN CAR
WISCONSIN BOY DRAGGED 2 MILES BY SCHOOL BUS

For a while after Iggy's diagnosis he had clipped such stories, a collector of misfortunes, as if this might lessen his pain. (*I cry because I have not shoes,* his grandmother used to say, *and then I see a man which has not feet.*) And for a while—he knew he should be ashamed of this, but fuck it—it had helped.

That night in their motel room, after a McDonald's meal Clio would never have allowed, Iggy slept with the AAA TripTik under her arm, as she had every night since they'd left Pittsburgh. She couldn't read a map yet, but Andrew had shown her in the atlas at home the route they would take—across Pennsylvania, up through New York and Connecticut, to Boston—to the special doctors. Their fingers, his and Iggy's, had traveled farther, all the way up the coast of Maine, to Rogue Bluff Harbor. The brash, bright, rocky headland where he'd spent childhood summers with his grandmother while his pediatrician parents treated more deserving children in the high plains of Peru. Iggy had never seen Baba, who'd died a decade before she was born, or Maine, or the ocean. The Main Ocean, Iggy called it, and would accept no substitutes; so they had not stopped along the coast after they'd turned north outside New York City.

Andrew stripped to his boxers and got into the too-wide bed next to Iggy's with a bottle of Glenlivet and one of the motel's plastic glasses. He jabbed the remote. The blowing up of a thirteenth-century bridge near Sarajevo was followed by an interview with various celebrities about AIDS, in which a French supermodel, eyes intermittent behind Lhasa Apso hair, declared, "*Moi, je suis contre.*" Andrew flicked it off and lay open-eyed in the dark. Sounds of other TVs, other transients, came to him dimly on the fruity, disinfected air.

Before the birth of Iggy, there had been, though he and Clio didn't realize it then, only small things. An accident on I-76, but no one was hurt; periodic layoffs from the Youngstown Philharmonic, in which Andrew, last-hired oboe, was usually the first player to go; the Porsche's first engine caught fire. ("Americans, *schätzchen*," Baba said—she was still alive then—"Americans have always the mechanical problems. For them *this* is tragedy.") After Iggy, everything changed. For the first few hours they had not seen: neither he nor Clio had been around babies much, and the newborn Grace slept all the time. The obstetrician and the pediatrician came to Clio's hospital room together to break the news, two men who looked so much alike (round, youngish, thinning hair) that Andrew thought of them ever afterward as the Tweedles, Dum and Dee. The baby, they said, had been born without the nerve that controls smiling and frowning. Moebius syndrome, it was called. An inherited disorder.

While they waited through Grace's first year to see whether she was retarded—a possible accompaniment of Moebius syndrome—Andrew did research. Shadyside Middle School, where he taught music, was on the bus line to the Carnegie-Mellon Library. In the waning winter afternoons he found his way to the *Encyclopedia of Birth Defects* and *Jablonski's Dictionary of Medical Syndromes*, paging through horrors, his dreams at night filled with the cleft faces of babies that looked as if they'd been pulled and twisted like taffy.

From the time he was Iggy's age, Baba had not made him hold her hand. Planting his feet in rubber boots on the stony bluff, he'd squint out past the lone pine to where the water seemed motionless, a jellied gleam beneath the sunrise that stained the dark-blue sky. Seagulls circled overhead. Baba knew their precise latitude, knew what was opposite if they could have seen three thousand miles to landfall. Andrew kept forgetting, preferring to imagine he looked across to Cornwall, caparisoned in sunrise colors, home of Merlin and King Arthur (he was reading already, greedily, the way an only child reads). He and Baba would stand side by side, listening to the gulls' austere cries, until the sun was all the way up.

At the end of one of those summers, his parents (returning from Peru) had explained to him the Quechua idea of time. We see the future ahead, the past behind, his father said; they see the opposite. The past is ahead of them, because it is known; the unknown future is behind their backs.

Things he could show her:

- Baba's tide pool below the bluff: the tiny, delicate, nearly transparent ghost crabs that tickled your ankles
- the place under the blue Atlas cedar where he'd awakened one morning to the birth of a hundred miniscule blond spiders in the web that trembled by his head
- snakelocks anemones
- the cove notched into the rocky bluff where they could swim, the two of them, in the seaweedy sun-warmed water

The motel clerk was spraying the plants—a sinewy yellowed palm and some ferns—with an atomizer bottle that made a malicious spitting sound. Iggy perched on a wrought-iron railing that served no visible purpose, her long legs dangling down, barefoot.

"Daddy!" she cried joyfully.

"Where have you been?" Relief made Andrew shout. He'd awakened in his chair in broad daylight to an empty room. Iggy regarded him with those root beer eyes, her mother's eyes.

"Right here, Daddy." The quaver in her voice was like a reed gone soft.

The clerk stopped pumping her atomizer to look at Andrew reproachfully. Except for the tattoo, she had a face like plain shiny crockery, a broad, untroubled brow. Plump: his seventh graders would have called her a jelly doughnut.

Iggy had on the orange-and-yellow-flowered top of her bathing suit and an old red corduroy skirt that was too short for her. Clio had let her do her own packing.

Andrew said, more gently, "Your feet are dirty, Ig." Iggy's shoulders loosened and her chin dropped: signs of relief.

"I'll cut them off," she offered cheerfully. "There'll be blood all over your carpet, Natalie. It'll soak in, in big puddles. Blood and mud and—"

"Stop it!" cried Andrew. But Iggy was laughing, and the clerk—so it was Natalie now, was it?—laughed with her. She came over and gave Iggy a spritz from her bottle and they laughed harder. Natalie didn't seem to notice how weird it was, laughter emerging from that frozen face, as if someone were playing the wrong sound track. Apparently, while Andrew slept, some accord had been reached.

He sat down on one of several brown plastic chairs that resembled large crouching insects. The room smelled like burned toast. A canary sang in a cage by the door, C-sharp/D-sharp, drilling into the headache left by last night's scotch. Jelly Doughnut's reproach was well-deserved, Andrew thought. He drank too much, spent too much, drove too fast. But Iggy didn't care about any of that. Andrew picked up the last crumbling Danish from a platter depicting Elizabeth Taylor in *Cat on a Hot Tin Roof*.

"Hey, Ig! Want some breakfast?"

"I ate already, Daddy."

"I gave her cereal and OJ, Mr. Rogers. She ate it all, *and* a bear claw. She was wicked hungry."

"Rogacz. Like 'catch.' Iggy threw up last night. She shouldn't've had that stuff."

Natalie, plastic spray bottle cradled in one arm like an Uzi, looked pointedly at the Danish in Andrew's hand. Iggy jumped off the railing and began twirling, arms outstretched, in a patch of morning sunlight. Natalie said, "Hey, don't bitch me out. I was trying to help, you know?"

Andrew thought, My daughter does not need *befriending*, for Chrissake. Natalie the Interloper got busy brushing crumbs from the continental breakfast onto the floor. The back of her yellow T-shirt said, "Let the Bastards Fall." He swallowed the last of his Danish and went in search of the men's room.

The future of America is in your hands (at eye level as he stood before the urinal, unzipping). *No more Bush shit. YOUR mom was pro-life!!!*

Why did he get angry each time as if it were the first, when by now he had it down to an algorithm? Surprise, hesitation, try again. Then (your choice) incomprehension/sympathy/ridicule. The kids at her school had already begun (it was only October) to call his daughter "Iggy Ugly." But ridicule wasn't necessarily the worst thing. One of the mothers in the support group he and Clio went to had been driven nearly out of her mind by well-meaning strangers running after her to say that her little boy had his arm caught in his sleeve. Convert your anger into action, the therapist said; think of yourself as a turbine. But Doctor Chumley (Our Chum, Clio called him) had two healthy sons. What did he know? What action was Andrew supposed to take here — pepper half the butts in Saint Perpetua's first grade with buckshot?

The paper towel dispenser was empty. He punched it, hard.

Back in their room — he'd left Iggy teasing the canary with Natalie's feather-duster — Andrew stood over their open suitcases. He tucked Iggy's copy of *Lizards in Color* into a side pocket, then pulled it out again. They should leave now, if they were to get back to Pittsburgh by Friday, as he'd promised Clio. He and Iggy were both cutting school to make this trip. A week before she was supposed to take Iggy to Boston,

Clio had broken her leg on a Sierra Club photo shoot in the Nittany Mountains; when it became clear Andrew would have to be the one to take Iggy to Mass General, he'd cashed in the plane tickets. He hated flying.

Reaching for Iggy's hair-clogged brush, he stopped. He pulled the Glenlivet from its nest of underwear and took a long swallow. The thought of getting in the car and going west, going home, made him feel leaden. He thought, We'll take a few more days; we'll go up to Maine. I'll show Iggy Rogue Bluff and Baba's grave and the ocean.

The first time he dialed his own number, he got the recorder. He hung up without leaving a message and dialed again: their signal for when something was urgent. This time Clio picked up.

Soft, at first. Reasonable. "Listen, A. We already thrashed this out. She needs the operation, and she needs it now. Before she gets too far in school, and the other kids . . . Before she can't get out from under the *label*."

Her soft voice made Andrew think of the soft slope of her belly under her green sweater, the weight she'd never lost after Iggy. Her voice had an almost unnoticeable tremolo, like the shimmer of extra flesh all over her body.

"Clio, she doesn't want it. If you'd seen her, with the surgeon. She wouldn't talk to me all the way down from Boston."

"You always think you know what she's feeling. But a lot of the time it's just what *you're* feeling." Soft, soft; but underneath, iron. "You want to keep her tied to us forever?"

Andrew was silent.

"Did she cry?"

"No." Immediately he wished he had lied.

"Well, is she upset now? How is she now?"

"She threw up last night." No need to mention dancing in the sunshine, laughing with the adhesive Natalie. "Clio. I think we should wait."

"We've *been* waiting. We could've had this operation when she was four. You said, six. Now she's six, and you say, eight. When she's eight, you'll say—"

"Clio—"

"No! I mean it, A. It must've been some twenty-four-hour bug, if she's okay now." Clio's voice cracked; he heard her take a breath. "Bring her straight back. She's going to miss too much school as it is. I'll see you Friday night."

Andrew sank down onto the bed, holding the dead receiver. He felt a trill along his spine, like cold fingers playing scales on his vertebrae. When Clio got like this, she never yielded. After they found out about the baby, during that awful year of tests, gristle had entered her soul bit by bit, until she became like the *mala mujer* his parents used to tell him about: the mythical Quechua woman hard and impious and alone as any man. Clio had no problem turning feeling into action; Doctor Chumley's advice had not been addressed to her. Over the years Andrew had seen her growing contempt for him, for his meek acceptance of Iggy. Yet she must have loved him once; they must have loved each other, because there was so much anger between them now.

Iggy burst into the room. Behind her, backlit by the morning sun, he glimpsed Natalie the Inescapable. For some reason, a reflex, he shot a quick look down at his fly. He opened his mouth to tell Iggy they were going to Maine, but she didn't give him a chance.

"Daddy! Natalie can take us! It's her afternoon off."

"Take us? Take us where?"

"To her secret place. It's wicked nice, Dad."

Andrew hesitated, about to say No. But this was the old Iggy restored to him, flushed and voluble, yesterday's silence forgotten.

"Please, Daddy, please, please." It came out *pleezh*. Iggy hopped on one foot, neatly, elegantly, the way she did when she knew she was going to get her wish, eyes alive in the still, small mask of her face.

The two of them were squaring off: the girl and Andrew. Hard to resist the exhilaration, the relief of having a target. Natalie sat beside him in a yellow slicker, the kind school crossing guards used to wear. The stiff glazed oilcloth crackled when she moved. It was raining steadily. On Natalie's lap Iggy made throaty little percussive clicks that sounded as if she were about to choke, a sound she'd learned as a baby would call her parents instantly to her crib.

"You okay, hon?" Natalie's sweet concern rebuked Andrew. Why get so involved with a stranger's kid? he wondered, not for the first time.

Natalie cranked down her window and the smell of recently deceased skunk, amplified by the rain-wet air, flooded in. "Fresh ear," she said to Iggy. "You think you're gonna hurl?"

Iggy shook her head.

The road, Wampanoag Parkway, twisted and turned, continually surprising Andrew. It was slicker than he'd expected, and they skidded taking a curve at the Porsche's usual speed. Natalie's breath drew in sharply. One for you, Jelly Doughnut, Andrew thought. When they were out of the skid, he accelerated sharply, pleased to feel her flinch. He glanced at the tach. Red-lining it.

Car Plunges Into River, Killing 3
4TH Wampanoag Fatality This Year

He slowed down.

They passed a billboard advertising one of the candidates for governor and exhorting voters to call 1-800-RI-ANGRY. Iggy missed that one.

She was too busy settling back, with a great crackling of oilcloth, into the curve of Natalie's arm. But she read the next two out loud (FOXY LADY—THE BEST IN TOPLESS; TOM FLURKEY USED CARS), along with several road signs. Natalie had to help her with the bumper sticker on the Toyota pickup that cut in front of them, demanding, in red letters on black, EQUAL RIGHTS FOR UNBORN WOMEN.

Rain streamed over the car's dusty windows, giving the world outside a filmy, romantic cast, like when Clio smeared vaseline over her portrait lens. The procession of used-car lots, auto body shops, and cheap chain restaurants gave way to farm stands heaped with pumpkins and zucchini whose colors sang in the rain. Then birch and hemlock, blond strands of pampas grass, a glimpse of the river. Here I am, Andrew thought, speeding down the fucking Wampanoag Parkway with Natalie the Ubiquitous. He kept his eyes on the road, his face expressionless.

"String bean mouth!" Iggy teased. She and Natalie giggled.

FACT: There are eighteen different kinds of smiles. FACT: A smile is produced by the action of two main muscles, the *Zygomaticus major* and the *Orbicularis oculi*. FACT: An artificially induced smile produces the same changes in the brain as a spontaneous one. A fake smile triggers feelings of joy.

Raise your cheeks.

Open your mouth.

Push the corners of your lips up.

Don's Depot Diner was a squat brick structure with a view of abandoned railroad tracks. Natalie assured Andrew it was the last place to eat before their still-mysterious destination. At Iggy's insistence, they sat at the counter. The only other customer was a young black policewoman at the other end reading *The Complete Book of Abs*. No sign of a waitress, much less of Don. Andrew tapped his menu on the countertop in 6/8 time. Carved in the worn wood was the declaration, *I ♥ Botto 4-evah.*

Iggy studied the boxes of breakfast cereal lined up along the counter. Natalie shrugged off her slicker, revealing a sleeveless blue cotton top that mercifully said nothing. She pulled the rubber band from her ponytail and shook it out. In the mirror behind the counter Andrew could see the dark-blonde hair under her arms, like tightly curled fiddlehead ferns. He saw how Iggy, between them, listed slightly toward Natalie. Iggy's red-brown hair, he noticed for the first time, was neatly combed; someone—of course, it must have been Natalie—had pulled it into a side-slung ponytail fastened with a purple tie. In the mirror Iggy's eyes met Natalie's. Natalie smiled.

It frightened Andrew to be so shut away from his daughter. Why had she attached herself to this Natalie? Why wouldn't she talk to him? From the moment yesterday when Doctor Zekai had begun speaking, he'd seen his daughter receding down a long corridor, dwindling, slowly but inexorably, into someone else. Someone he did not know. Embarrassed by the fear in his own mirrored eyes, Andrew looked quickly down at the counter. *I ♥ Iggy 4-evah.*

Forever: the sound of the word was a breath held and released, a wave curling and then rushing forward onto the sand. We could do it, he thought; and his heart took up a crazy 3/4 time. We could go forever. Keep going north. Maine, Rogue Bluff, the ocean, Canada. That's it, that's what I want. But what does *she* want?

Christ, what he wouldn't give for a single-malt Scotch, straight up. Iggy said, "Life is great. Life is so good."

Andrew pulled a paper napkin out of the dispenser and wiped a pearl of drool from each corner of her mouth. "Well, Ig, that's nice," he said insincerely. "I'm glad you're having a good time."

Iggy laughed. "No, Dad! I mean the *cereal.*"

• • • •

The three of them stood in the middle of a small, overgrown park over-looking the mouth of the river. Behind them was a dense half circle of birch and hemlock and scrub pine. In front of them was an abandoned carousel. Most of the animals, though worn and weathered, were still in place.

Iggy turned to her father, bright with wonder, and stretched out her arms. The waist-high wooden platform looked strong enough, no boards missing. Andrew lifted Iggy up and set her on it. Then he clambered up himself. On his knees, he turned to give a hand to Natalie, but she was already hauling herself aboard. She and Iggy scrambled to their feet and began to explore, hand in hand. The rain had stopped. The carousel's canopy trapped a heavy mist rising from the river, and in the foggy afternoon light their figures quickly blended with the unearthly shapes of the animals.

"Be careful!" Andrew called after them.

The cool, wet air was fragrant with pine and rotting leaves and the salt smell of the ocean, invisible on the far side of the river. Andrew put a hand on the flank of a prancing horse and pulled himself upright to follow the girls, weaving in and out between the animals. They were set three abreast, in staggered rows: not only horses, but other creatures as well. An elephant, one tusk broken off; a tiger; a horned goat; a giraffe with a snake coiled around its neck; an ostrich. They tossed their heads, arched their necks, pawed and pranced and leapt. He was wandering through a forest of frozen motion. The colors of the intricately carved trappings, dulled by time and weather, evoked dim Arthurian echoes. White for innocence, he remembered; gold for nobility, blue for truth.

Iggy and Natalie were sitting side by side on a wide-seated chariot borne by dragons. Iggy jumped to her feet and said, "Daddy! Up me!" A phrase from babyhood.

Her face when he seated her on a rearing horse went pink with pleasure. She stroked the long skull with one hand while the other held tight to the metal pole. Her horse's ears were laid back, its lip curled in a majestic snarl. Where the glittering glass eyes would have been were only empty sockets. Iggy patted the carved curls of its mane. "You, Daddy," she said. "*You* get up!"

Andrew shook his head, walked back and sat down in the dragon chariot next to Natalie. All he wanted, suddenly, was to be still. To sit surrounded by these marvelous beasts and look out across the river, as he and Baba used to look out across the ocean. To sit and think what he should do.

Natalie's oilcloth crackled. She said, "This whole pack useta belong to my family. Prospect Pack. This merry-go-round was wicked beautiful, back then. My great-grandpa useta repaint it every September. We've got pitchers of it at home."

Andrew leaned back in their chariot and looked around him. He imagined the bright, ingratiating colors the animals had once been: cobalt, magenta, chartreuse, scarlet. Colors with kingly names. He preferred them as they were now, truculent, wintry, with all their imperfections. Iggy, five or six yards ahead, leaned and whispered into her horse's ear. The river was a blind, dull green. Gulls hung in the air, level with the carousel, then glided away. Their cries were the sound of remembering.

"That was before he got poor. In the Depression, you know? This pack—the bank, like, took it. It was wicked unfear."

Andrew's headache had lifted. He felt a loosening, looking out over the river, the sounds and smells of this place so real after the series of small closed spaces, the car, the motel rooms. He felt a widening, an ease, as if he himself were opening out. The feeling he used to have standing on the bluff with Baba.

"People came on the train from all over. From Worcester, even. My family was, like, famous."

Why was she telling him all this? He just wanted to sit quietly, in this place where anything seemed possible, and think. Massachusetts, Maine, the ocean, Canada. *Wer jetzt kein Haus baut*, Baba used to say. Who builds no house now, shall never have one. What he had in mind might be kidnapping. (Could you nap your own kid?) And what would they live on, he and Iggy?

"Natalie. Hey, Nat! Come on—get up here!"

"Not now, hon. In a minute. Mr. Rogue-Axe," Natalie said carefully. "I know what you're doing."

Andrew turned to look at her then. Her plump, plain face regarded him earnestly, the rose tattoo incongruous as a kiss. She could have been one of his older seventh graders, the ones who'd been left back a couple of times. Her feet in heavy, black Doc Martens scuffed at the wooden platform.

"What do you mean?"

"I know you and Iggy are, like, on the run. Iggy told me. She says you're gonna escape, so she don't have to have her operation."

On the run. It had a ring to it. It made his heart rise, like a conductor's uplifted baton.

"So what?" There was a pole growing out of the head of Andrew's dragon. Exhilarated, he gripped the cold metal. "So what, Natalie?"

"I want to go with you."

"What? Are you crazy?"

"Look, Mr. Rogue-Axe-"

"Rogacz."

"Mr. Rogacz. I gotta get away. They're all bunbrains and mall doofs here. See what I'm sayin'?" Her voice speeded up, urgent, persuasive. "You can leave me off in New York City."

He looked up ahead at Iggy. She stopped digging her heels, in imaginary spurs, into the flank of her horse. She was listening.

Massachusetts, Maine, the ocean, Canada.

Natalie leaned toward him. "I've got money. I wouldn't be a burden or anything. Take me with you." Her tone shifted from plea to threat. "If you don't—"

"No," Andrew said loudly. "We're not going to New York."

Iggy turned to look at him, slinging one leg around so that she sat side-saddle, head tilted the way she did when she wasn't sure what something meant. Her hands held each other by the wrist. Andrew knew he was asking her to choose. For a terrifying moment he wondered who would be saving whom. Then he took a deep breath of piney, almost-ocean air.

"We're not going to New York. Are we, Sweetpea? We're going to Maine. To the Main Ocean."

Iggy looked at him for a long second. Then her hands released each other. Her face, unmoving, tightened all over with delight.

At last, at last, he had reached her.

Biscuit Baby ❀

FROM THE TRAM WINDOW THE LENIN HILLS APPEAR TO BE SWATHED in gauze. Snow-covered ice crawls from the granite embankment of the Moskva River toward its center, down which a lone barge creeps. From its smokestack a hopeful spume rises, whiter than white, into the iron dusk. The tramful of warm bodies, the smell of sweat and onions, make it hard to breathe. Vera tries to will herself out into the deepening twilight, into the city, with its bare black trees and golden domes. She's on her way to the Ministry of the Interior, where she has an appointment with a deputy administrator, the one investigating the whereabouts of her husband, Mitya. For nearly a year now she's had no word, not even the most delayed of letters. At last she left Paris and came back to look for him.

This inquiry is the final one in Vera's search, the last resort. After it she'll see her daughter—*their* daughter—Galya. Her heart lifts at the thought. It's been two months now since they've seen each other. Moscow is the safest place in the Soviet Union right now—more food than the countryside, farther from the advancing German lines than Leningrad—so Vera left Galya here, with her aunt and uncle, while she searched for Mitya. Aunt Nadezhda—with her wide, upholstered bosom and arms that never tremble, and the gold tooth that winks in the shadow of her smile—Aunt Nadezhda tells bedtime stories, tales of Old Russia in which princely steeds speak and toss their gleaming heads. Galya at four is crazy about horses.

The *babushka* beside Vera snorts loudly, then wipes her nose on her coat sleeve. Vera closes her eyes and pictures Galya—two tight, molasses-colored braids straining her hair back from her shining forehead (too much forehead for a little girl). At night, unbraided, her hair flows rippling to her waist.

When Vera was four, she had the same long braids. In Odessa, in 1916. There they were, the whole family, at the edge of the Black Sea, where spent waves the color of spit tasted their toes. There they were: Papa, nose coated with white zinc ointment; the cousins in various poses of pre-adolescent worldliness; Mama standing beside Vera, squinting westward into the sun. Seaweed attacked Vera's ankles and she threw her arms around her mother's waist. "*Mamechka!*" she cried.

There they were, Vera and her cousins, playing *Pryg-Skok* in damp woolen bathing suits sticky with sand, running in a pack through the dusty twilight, creeping out at night to rattle dice in a cup by the light of a beeswax candle.

With a series of long, jolting shudders, the tram halts. "Out of service, citizens!" shouts the conductress. Everyone crowds to the doorway and descends into the bitter night. The Ministry of the Interior is on Gorky Street, several blocks away. Vera begins to walk along a makeshift path of snow-slick, uneven boards, peering up at the street names set high in the stone walls. Gassy yellow light from the streetlamps makes them waver and change.

Vera can feel the cold seeping through her felt boots. Her fingers ache, and she shoves her hands deep into her coat pockets. Her anxiety about the interview with the deputy administrator has momentarily vanished; all she wants is to be warm again.

. . . .

By the spring of 1926 Vera and her southern-reared mother and aunts
and uncles (except for Uncle Fyodor, who got out to France in 1919)
had all left Odessa and made their way, one by one, to Moscow—all
except her father, who died fighting with the Whites in 1918. Moscow
was a cold, clamoring city where none of them ever managed to feel at
home. Vera's mother died that autumn, of homesickness compounded
by hunger, and Aunt Nadezhda inherited fourteen-year-old Vera.

A decade passed. Vera's childhood at the edge of the Black Sea
melted to a memory, then a dream. Pregnant, with a husband in the
camps, and mildly deranged from lack of food, Vera walked through
frozen streets to the Kiev Station and waited three days and nights for a
train going south. There would not be one—citizens farther west had
pulled up too many of the ties for firewood—but none of those waiting
knew that. "Here we are, then!" Uncle Anton cried hearteningly, when
he found her among the shawled and greatcoated forms that stretched
along the platform like endless piles of used clothing. "*Slava Bogu!*"
Thank God.

In the hospital the oxygen mask came down over her face, and
"Breathe!" they said, "Breathe deep, now!" She thought, They're lying.
"You'll fall asleep now," the midwife said, but Vera knew: This is death,
I'm dying.

Afterwards, lying awake in the hard hospital bed, she was so sore
she could barely move. From down the hall came the muted minia-
ture howls of babies. Whispered stories in the dark ward; rain on the
dark windows like the silver beads on her mother's evening dress, long
ago; the smell of blood, and soft-boiled eggs.

The deputy administrator is fat and pale, with small black eyes like
raisins in dough. From time to time he coughs into a grimy handkerchief.

"Your husband died approximately one year ago," he says, in an administrative voice, a voice from which all feeling has been purged. "In the autumn . . ." He pauses, looks down at some documents on his desk. "in . . . October, 1939. In the transit camp in Tarascan . . . from, ah . . . tuberculosis."

He rises, stands behind his desk. "My condolences, citizeness." One hand holds the handkerchief to his mouth; he does not extend the other to Vera.

She studies those raisin eyes. With the handkerchief to his face the deputy administrator looks like a bandit. He's lying, she thinks. Improvising the details: time, place, manner of death. The papers on his desk probably have nothing to do with Mitya. But somehow she knows that what he says is, nevertheless, true.

Mitya is dead. She can feel it.

It speaks to her in the November wind that stirs the bare branches of the trees outside the ministry, in the hollow clang of the bell as the trolley lurches forward on its way to Aunt Nadezhda, in the whistling onion-scented breath of the man sitting next to her. Mitya is dead. They can no longer take him away from her, or from the daughter he has never seen. Mitya is in Russia now, for always.

Summer, 1937. Paris. Prosperous Uncle Fyodor managed to buy their escape, Vera's and her baby's.

"*Slava Bogu!*" the other émigrés said to each other, fanning themselves in the soft, dense shade of the chestnut trees in the Parc des Buttes-Chaumont. "Thank God! We are lucky!"

Galya wore a diaper and a pinafore that smelled coolly of starch. In the park they sat on an afghan on the grass, the baby's upturned face serious as a pansy. Eight months old, well-fed now, *du lait, du fromage, des fraises du bois.* (These things hold down one corner of the afghan.)

"You are lucky, Vera Ivanovna. Lucky."

This baby was plump, solid, earthbound. Her flesh, warmed by months of sun, is the golden-brown of a nearly-done biscuit. *"Mon petit biscuit,"* Vera murmured in the new language, nuzzling her, and then, more softly, in the old one: *"Moja piroshka!"* The baby was propped against her—she'd only just begun to sit up by herself—and she began to slide. Vera put both arms around her—clumsily, awkwardly, but she held on. She held on hard to the biscuit baby, as if she might rise and float away.

Walking in the cold and dark, over the corrugated frozen mud of Vavilova Street toward Aunt Nadezhda's, feels like falling. Vera does not know if what she feels is grief. Mitya has been lost to her for so long now. How can she not be accustomed to his absence? She stumbles, saves herself by grabbing hold of a lamppost. The street is so dark. *Breathe!* they said. *Breathe deep, now!* She gulps wildly, mouthfuls of cold, cinder-scented air.

Pedestrians push past, *babushkas* with bulging string bags, men in dark coats, women holding children by the end of their knotted woolen scarves. It's begun to snow. Vera sticks out her tongue to catch some, the way Galya likes to do. She can't feel the flakes landing, only the faint taste, a kiss of iron, they leave behind.

1939. By the end of her third year in Paris, Vera was more homesick than she would ever have thought possible. Could one be homesick for a home that was gone, destroyed, and most of the town along with it? Homesick for the missing? The dead?

In the Parc des Buttes-Chaumont she saw Galya, no longer a baby but a little girl now, catch her lower lip between her teeth the way Mitya used to do. "Silly pigeon!" Galya cried. "He talks French, not Moscow. Like you, Mama."

There were leaves on the ground—it was October—and she seized

Galya's hand and together they dove into a great fragrant pile of them, dry and sharp, with a loamy dampness at its heart. The smell of the birch woods outside the *dacha* in those long-ago autumns, when Vera was small. Before they left Odessa. Before hunger, before thirst, before the night-long rattle of gunshot outside shuttered windows.

Uncle Anton and Aunt Nadezhda live in a two-room flat on a long avenue of decaying stone buildings massed, fortresslike, together. Here it is, No. 29. It's dark and shuttered, a far cry from when it was built, two wars and a revolution ago. The outer door is unlocked. Vera walks in out of the cold, past the bronze-and-mahogany elevator doors that have been boarded shut since 1926, up the winding stairs.

About to raise her hand, to bang her knuckles, sore with cold, against the peeling door of the apartment, she pauses.

The door opens. There is Aunt Nadezhda in her black beaded dress, her familiar smell of mothballs and Siberian tobacco. Aunt Nadezhda's bright squirrel-eyed gaze falters as she takes in Vera's expression.

"Verochka! Oh, my poor little dove. He is dead?"

Vera's silence fills the little hallway.

Fear turns Aunt Nadezhda's red face redder as she understands, it's worse than that. "The exit visas. Yours and Galya's. You did get them?"

Vera hesitates—for this fraction of a second, there can still be hope—then shakes her head. And though she hasn't admitted it, will never admit it, her aunt knows. She knows the reason Vera has no exit visas is because she refused to ask for them. Because she chose to stay here, with Mitya.

"*Durak!*" her aunt will say, in a voice hoarse with despair. You fool.

In the room beyond, with its carved wooden chests and icons of cross-looking saints and worn rugs laid one over another, Vera sees that the table has been set with the old damask cloth. There's a bottle of vodka and little gold-rimmed cups like thimbles. Black bread, a platter of sliced beets, another of cucumber and scallions, and in the exact center, under the ceiling light, a pyramid of hard-boiled eggs, peeled and gleaming. The samovar chuckles in its corner.

Galya comes running in from the next room, galloping like one of her beautiful bedtime steeds, her face alight.

"*Mamechka!*" she cries.

Thoreau's Laundry ✤

T HE MORNING'S FIRST CLIENT—SHE NEVER CALLED THEM PATIENTS
—appeared on the list as Junius Johns. This was followed by the
usual basics: M, 8, left ear, AA. Sex, age, presenting problem, origin
(auto accident). In the margin a penciled notation from Edwin, her
receptionist, read: "Mad Mom + Relatives."

Celia put her elbows on the desk and let her forehead sink onto
her palms. She was tired. Not just tired—weary. Simon's catheter had
gone AWOL at one in the morning, and they'd spent the rest of the
night in the ER. (How many nights did that make, now? How many
hours?) Noise and cold and too-bright lights and too-bright student
doctors. Repeating her husband's history, over and over, to a succession
of twelve-year-olds in lab coats and stethoscopes. Her husband in pain,
and nothing in the world she could do about it. By the time Doctor
Mikhailov entered the cubicle and took Simon's hand between both of
his, the sun was up. A cautious November sun that barely reddened the
sky above the parking lot, where the cold fell like a blessing on Celia's
hospital-hot face and winter birds measured out early-morning sounds
in the trees overhead. She called Leslie on her cell phone and asked
her to meet Simon's ambulance at the house when they'd finished
with him ("No prob!" That was Leslie, best friend ever, and Celia's
cousin to boot. "I'll call you and let you know he's okay, okay?") Then

she drove straight to the office, where wonderful Edwin had had a cappuccino and croissant waiting.

Celia brushed the silky crumbs off her desk and opened the drawer where she kept an assortment of puppets for child clients. Though usually the adults needed the distraction more. To Celia's continuing surprise, people found what she did for a living grisly. Maxillofacial prosthetist: that was the official name, the phrase her accountant put at the top of each page of her income tax return. She made eyes and ears and noses—and any other parts of a face that might be needed—for people who were missing them. People whom cancer or fire or gunshot had ravaged. People whom the plastic surgeons had given up on.

She took out the first puppet she touched and pulled it on over her left hand, wriggling her thumb and little finger into the arms, comforted by the feel of velvet. An ancient, bearded little man in a midnight-blue gown scattered with gold stars, and a pointed magician's cap. When she crooked her index finger, he nodded. She buzzed Edwin, two shorts: *Ready*.

The door opened. A gaggle of female voices. Then a wheelchair appeared—really a sort of wheeled chaise lounge, containing a small black boy with both legs outstretched—flanked by three large women in flowing flowered smocks, all talking at once.

"—you *know* he never—"

"I'm just sayin'—"

"—that's what *any*body gotta—"

Behind this procession Edwin hovered, rolling his eyes. Celia put up her hands and shouted, "Stop!"

Instant silence, followed, inexplicably, by giggles. The largest of the three women, standing beside the wheelchair in magenta silk, put a hand across her mouth.

"You must be Junius," Celia said to the boy. "I'm Celia."

The boy's eyes, large and liquid, met hers for a heartbeat, then shifted to the puppet. His left leg wore a cast from hip to ankle; the right was bare, except for a layer of what looked like raw chopped meat spread all along his thigh. The harvest site for a skin graft, Celia knew. The surgeon who'd referred Junius believed in old-fashioned gauze dressings soaked in iodoform.

"He don't talk hardly at all, doctor," the woman in magenta said. "Since the accident."

"I'm not a doc—"

"Barely a peep!" cried one of the other women, and the third chimed in, "Lord knows!"

Edwin brought two more chairs from the outer office, and the women sat down in a flurry of silk, Magenta beside the wheelchair, Carnation and Tiger Lily behind it. Edwin cocked his head, and his eyebrows (so black and perfect that she'd always wondered if he penciled them) rose. This was as far as he went with worrying about her, which was why she'd looked for a male secretary in the first place. There were too many concerned females in her life already. Celia mouthed *Thanks*, and he left, closing the door behind him.

Celia turned to Magenta. "Mrs. Johns? I understand you're—"

The woman leaned forward. "The hospital made us come here," she said, spitting the words. Edwin had been right, as usual: this woman was mad. "The *in*surance made us. No more surgery—that's what they say. My boy don't show promise. He ain't a *candidate*."

"Whatever *that* means," Carnation said, and Tiger Lily added, "Lord knows!"

Celia sighed. This Greek chorus was going to get old fast. The length of Junius's wheelchair put the whole group at a slightly theatrical distance from her desk. Junius himself sat chewing gum with downcast eyes. When his jaw moved, the hole where his left ear should have been pulsed faintly. She was always surprised at how small the aural opening actually was.

She rose and went around the desk and crouched down next to him, on his left side. He didn't look up. She raised the puppet in front of his face and bent her thumb to make it bow. "I'm Merlin!" she said, in a deep, plummy voice. "I make magic."

The boy's mouth twitched. He raised his head, but he didn't look at Celia, only at the puppet.

"Can't see what good playin' dolls gonna do. Or false ears, either. The Lord alone can help my boy now."

"Lord help him!"

"Yeah, Lord!"

Celia turned her head and shot the three women a look—what Simon called her dark-blue look—useful in ER waiting rooms. There was a subsiding rustle of silk around three sets of knees. Then, silence.

Inches now from Junius's head, she had a good view. Stumpy petals of flesh ringed the aural opening, where the lobe and helix had been sheared away; only the tragus remained. A webbing of scar tissue made the skin look like hammered bronze. It wasn't ugly; it just didn't look like an ear. She saw exactly where Doctor Prout would implant the gold-and-titanium abutments her silicone ear would snap onto. (She wouldn't mention that now; better to leave breaking the news about more surgery to the surgeon.) Junius had stopped chewing gum, and she could feel him trembling. His hand gripped her wrist.

"Ho!" she said, in Merlin's voice. "You look like a fine, strong lad. A good candidate for magic."

She felt the boy stiffen.

"We don't believe in magic," his mother said. "We believe in Jesus."

Celia looked up. The woman smiled, not apologetically but as if to say, *You'll never understand, so don't even try.* A feeling Celia knew well.

Junius said nothing.

Celia rose and went around to the boy's right to look at his good ear. The one she would make for him had to match this one, imperfections and all. She noted the wrinkle where the lobe attached, the too-sharply folded helix that gave the top a Spock-like point. Black skin was harder to match than white: she'd start with umber and burnt sienna, maybe add a little monastral red.

She felt the boy's breath, with its smell of spearmint, graze her cheek. She thought, This at least is something I can do.

The evening air was full of unshed rain. In the thickening darkness a sea-smelling wind stirred the few leaves left on the trees. Homeward, she drove more slowly than she needed to. Headlights loomed suddenly behind her, slewed sideways, shot past, loomed again.

Simon would be waiting for her in the ground-floor sunporch-turned-sickroom. Would this be a good night, or a bad?

Low, womanly hills replaced the clustered lights of the city. Celia turned the heat up. At the junction where 101 split off from Route 6 she looked for the turkey that lived on the triangle of grass there, in the glow of the floodlighted sign announcing the Township of Jerimoth. For the last few years there'd been an overabundance of turkeys in rural areas. She peered through the smoky blue twilight. *If it paces past, Simon won't be mean. If it turns its head toward me, he will.*

Multiple sclerosis had made their marriage a ménage à trois. It was as simple, as complicated, as that.

"You have lucky eyes and a high heart."

The first thing Simon ever said to her, that June night eighteen

years ago. (My Shakespeare professor, her cousin Leslie had said, dragging Celia the length of the lantern-lit veranda, their long taffeta skirts
rustling. He's totally gorgeous, you've *got* to meet him.) Behind them
the orchestra began tuning up, quick interrogative sounds.

"Dance with me. Every dance. With me."

Impossibly romantic; but then, *they'd* been impossibly romantic.
Impossibly young (her). Impossibly married (him). So impossible that
they had to happen.

Her key stuttered in the lock, reluctance made physical. There was the
breath-held moment—every night, now—*What will I find?* (Husband
on the floor, blood pooling under his temple; husband sprawled head-
first down the steps to the basement; husband slumped sideways in his
wheelchair, raising a book upside-down in his good hand to shelter
tears of fury.) She forced the key all the way in, pushed open the heavy
oak door.

"Seal? That . . . you?"

His words were halting but clear, his voice strong enough to
carry across the living room. Celia's breath escaped through dry lips.
Relieved, she bent to pick up the mail from the floor below the mail
slot. Electric bill, gas bill, various catalogues, a flyer from the MS Society's Well Spouse Group.

Simon looked up as she paused in the archway between the living
room and the sunporch. For an instant his face wore the expression
she remembered from years ago—from all those meetings-after-long-
absence, in those first years before they'd been able to marry—*I'm so
glad to see you.*

The tip of his tongue touched his mustache, then retreated. "How
was . . . your day?"

His eyes crinkled at the corners with the old wryness. Simon's sense of the absurd was the thing, besides sex, that had made her fall for him in the (impossible) first place.

Relief brought the itch of tears to her throat. She swallowed. "Fine. How was yours? What's new?"

"New York. New . . . Jersey."

"New . . . Mexico," they said, in unison.

Eighteen years together, eight of them healthy: Professor Simon Feldstein had taught her a few things. Some Yiddish words, how to make risotto, quite a few lines from Shakespeare, and a way of joking that kept you from falling off the edge of the world. Celia kissed him lightly on the mustache, threw her parka over a chair, handed him the remote. The sound of the Weather Channel followed her into the kitchen.

A good night, then. In a way, the bad nights were easier. The good nights made her remember. The good nights disarmed her.

And, yes, you ARE *above the freezing mark, Providence, but it sure doesn't* FEEL *like that!*

Celia opened the freezer and peered inside. The phone rang.

When she picked up, her mother's voice demanded, "Where *were* you?"

"God, Mom—I'm sorry. I forgot all about lunch. Something came up. An emergency."

"Simon? What happened? Is he—"

"Not Simon." Celia took out a frozen dinner and let the freezer door slam shut on her lie. "A client."

"Because if it was Simon—"

"Mom! Simon's okay—he's fine. So, what did *you* do this afternoon? Teeth?" Her mother's current lover, whom Leslie had christened the Priapodontist, was in the middle of replacing her entire lifetime accumulation of fillings with gold.

"Nothing. After lunch you and I were supposed to go shopping."
(And how she loved it, Celia thought: The cries of What?-You're-her-
mother? Bridling and beaming.) "You know, you'd look slimmer in
one of those new trumpet skirts. Maybe with a cropped sweater."

"I've got to go, Mom. Time for Simon's meds. I'll call you later."

She put her dinner in the oven, "Hungry Man" servings of fried
chicken and mashed potatoes and corn frozen in their own neatly
partitioned tinfoil tray, a depraved appetite she'd recently developed.
Then she began to grind the evening meds with a mortar and pestle.

From the day Simon had been diagnosed, almost eleven years
ago, her mother had made no secret of what she thought would be
best for everyone concerned. Simon in a nursing home; Celia with,
married or not, a real mate; Bess herself beamingly promoted, at long
last, to What?-You're-a-*grandmother?*-hood. It terrified Celia that her
mother's vision matched the one (the impossible one) that tattooed
itself across her closed eyelids every night as she lay awake in the bed
next to Simon's.

The medications, mingling and dissolving, smelled like sulfur.
When the powder was as fine as she could get it, she stirred it into a
beaker of warm water until it dissolved in a pastel cloud.

Colder air means BLACK ICE! *We'll have an update on that later
tonight.*

In the sunporch she turned off Simon's feeding pump and
detached it from the G-tube inserted in her husband's stomach, slowly
poured the meds solution into the G-tube, then hung a fresh bag of
liquid diet on his IV pole and hooked it up to the pump. "Chief . .
. nourisher . . . in life's feast," Simon murmured in his Shakespeare
voice. Celia reattached the feeding tube to the G-tube. Snapping them
together, she pulled too hard on the end that protruded from the pale,
freckled flesh of Simon's belly, and heard his sharp, in-drawn breath.
"Sorry!" she said.

He shook his head. "It's . . . okay."

She rose and turned the pump back on, stood listening for its slow, meditative clicks.

In the little bathroom she assembled the paraphernalia for his shot. Somehow, no matter how careful she was with things—G-tube, catheter, hypodermic—she always hurt him. The other Well Spouses in her support group never hurt their partners.

Kneeling beside Simon's wheelchair, she breathed in his familiar smell: baby powder, urine, and something less definable, the remote, forest odor of decay. *Okay.* Choose today's spot (there was a complicated rotation system involving arms, thighs, and belly), swab spot, insert fresh needle into holder, suck in sterile water 1.3 milliliters, inject water into ampule, turn ampule upside down until contents mix with water, suck in contents 1.3 milliliters (no air bubbles! flick with fingernail to disperse), hold needle poised in one hand, pinch husband's flesh between thumb and forefinger of other. People assumed Celia would be deft. Useless to protest that, even counting her prosthesis training from the VA a dozen years ago, she'd gone to art school, not med school. People didn't see the difference between handling something inert and handling something that breathed.

Our Little Marvel Snowblower does all this, and MORE!

Simon kept his eyes on the TV screen. The needle glittered in the lamplight. She plunged it in. He winced.

Celia let her breath out. That was it, until bedtime. She thought of these routines, collectively, as a sort of quilting stitch that held their pieced-together life in place. She didn't know how Simon viewed them.

Hug him, at least touch him. Give him his body back. Slowly she drew the palm of her hand across his neck, under his woolen shirt. The skin felt warm and grainy. His eyes closed in pleasure like a cat's. She gathered up her medical paraphernalia. In the bathroom she threw the used needle into the big red rubber Sharps container that squatted in one corner. The skull-and-crossbones on its belly leered at her.

At last she sat down next to Simon's wheelchair with Hungry Man on her lap and a glass of white Zinfandel on the table beside her. Two years ago, when the G-tube was inserted permanently into Simon's stomach, they'd agreed—or rather, Simon, with the generosity she remembered from the Well Years, had insisted—that they would still eat together. Now he watched her, and she let him: a gustatory voyeur.

His nose twitched. Wistfully?

"It tastes terrible," she assured him. "It tastes like . . . like breaded toilet paper and shoe buttons," and was rewarded with his brief bark of a laugh.

That's it for you folks in New England. Stay tuned for STORM STORIES!

Simon's good hand fumbled across the remote until it met the "Off" button. Silence. He said, "Cheers!"

She raised her glass in a toast to his IV pole and drank deeply, the wine stinging her throat. Then she told him about her day.

Bedtime was hoisting Simon up, coaxing the flesh together; was the weight of him, wheelchair to grab bars to commode to bed, thudding onto her shoulders and traveling down her spine; was the separate sigh from each of them when at last he lay, more or less straight, in the bed; was the cool gust from the down quilt as it settled over him; was the snap of the bedside light, extinguished.

Like putting a child to bed—the child they hadn't had. Plenty of time, they used to think.

Simon fell asleep quickly, the way he always did. Downstairs, Celia poured another glass of wine and settled into the sofa, settled into the part of the day that was hers, and thought about her lover.

Max.

Was it only a week ago they were hiking in Maine? Three hundred feet above the Atlantic, in a light snow, the path wound up and up between stony banks and pine trees, slippery and steep. When they came out, finally, onto the view of the shining little harbor at Rogue Bluff, it took her breath away. *Her* breath—not theirs. Max, who for the last half-hour had been a good twenty yards ahead, didn't stop to wait for her. To see this together: the sheer drop to the sea, the curve of the bay, the blue-green water with its flock of boats sheltering beneath the cliff. Where the path—rough stone steps now, winding down and down into the trees—continued, Max's square Scandinavian head and shoulders disappeared around a bend.

The following day, when she woke up, he was gone. Above her head the skylight in the conical cloth roof of the yurt showed a rose-colored sky. Sunrise. Warmth and light and emptiness. The woodstove glowed red; he'd stoked the fire. On the rough plank floor beside her sleeping bag he'd left a note.

Celia's cousin Leslie was the only person in her life who knew about Max. She'd met him in the spring, a few weeks after he and Celia had become lovers. The Contender, Leslie had christened him. He was the first one she'd ever liked. She had nicknames for all of Celia's lovers over the last decade: the Flake, the Field Marshal, Mr. Something-for-Nothing, the Thief of Joy. ("You said it, not me," Leslie told her when she protested this last one. "You said he ruined every good time.") Yet who, Celia wondered, could blame these men for not being able to handle what the Field Marshal used to call "the spouse issue"?

Leslie was the one who, whenever Celia got depressed about all this—whenever, over the past ten years, she'd referred to herself as the Well Slut—said, No.

"You're trying to make a life out of the pieces you have, Seal. That's all anybody ever does. It's just, your pieces are harder to fit together than most."

The afternoon's first call was her mother. Celia wedged the phone between her ear and her shoulder and looked over the appointment schedule Edwin had just laid on her desk. "Read any good books lately?" she said into the phone. Bess read two or three at a time, putting one down and picking up another, the way a chain smoker smoked.

"At the moment I'm reading the biography of Thoreau Leslie gave me for my birthday. And I'm in the middle of that fantastic new book, *Geyser Life*. Don't change the subject. Are you gaining weight?"

"*Guys Are Life*? I don't *think* so."

"No, no. *Geyser Life*. Old Faithful, and all that. Great photographs. You could do worse, Cecilia."

"Worse photographs?"

"Worse than give men a place in your life."

If you only knew, Celia thought. So many men; so little place.

"It wouldn't hurt Simon. He'd never know."

He *doesn't* know. And he never will. No one but Leslie will ever know about Max, or any of the others.

"You'd get out more. No wonder you're gaining weight. Thoreau said, 'Live the life you've imagined.' He said, 'Go confidently in the direction of your dreams.' Where do you ever go in the evenings, besides Well Spouse meetings?"

"We've been through this a hundred times. Listen, I can't talk right now. My one-thirty is out in the waiting room. The little boy, remember, the one who got hit by—"

"Cecilia—"

"Gotta go, Mom. Love you. Bye."

· · · ·

Celia's studio occupied half of the top floor of an old factory building in Pawtucket. Cold clear light poured in through the tall windows. The big, high-ceilinged room held the welcoming smells of plaster, paint, linseed oil. She turned on both space heaters, then took off her jacket and hung it on a peg by the door. The boom-box, tuned to an oldies station, drowned out the rap music from the painter's studio next door. A group Celia's mother had loved when Celia was in grade school sang about how hard life used to be. As always when she was in the studio, her spirits rose. Home ground: here she was deft, decisive, sure.

The mold for Mrs. de Carvalho had cured. Celia took a tiny jeweler's hammer from the tool rack above her worktable and began to tap the plaster around the edges. One of the first prostheses Celia had ever made, Mrs. de Carvalho's silicone eye—its pale green iris dusty with age, like the bloom on a grape—had had to be remade twice over the last twelve years, to keep pace with its aging mate.

She worked on the lashes most of the afternoon. It was a job requiring laser-like concentration, which Celia liked because of the peace it brought her. Nothing stilled obsessive rumination like the need to lift minute hairs, two or three at a time, in tiny tweezers the size of a needle, and punch them into the silicone eyelid at precisely the right angle, over and over. On the wall at the back of the worktable was a mirror about a foot wide, to which she held up the eye from time to time to get a fresh view. She worked until the eye, checked against photos of Mrs. de Carvalho's real one, had almost all the imperfections of its mate. The cornea and iris were excellent matches, but the sclera—she hadn't been able to get the precise mottling of yellow on white. She sighed. As if in commiseration, the radio began to play "I Can't Get No Satisfaction." Celia blew a few stray lash hairs off the eye, so lifelike she almost waited for it to blink, then put it into a gray plastic case and set it on the Outgoing Shelf. Perfect is the Enemy of

Good—that was what they'd taught at the VA. In the end you didn't so much finish a piece as abandon it.

The studio's many-paned windows gleamed with sunset. Feeling she'd earned a break, Celia took the cardboard box marked "JOHNS, J. 11/04" from the Pending Shelf. Junius's mother had cancelled his initial fitting yesterday, without explanation. Celia's disappointment had, she knew, been out of scale, almost to the point of tears. She'd made Edwin—eyebrows raised at the inappropriateness—phone Junius's house. There'd been no answer.

She wiped the surface of her worktable with a chamois, sweeping silicone fragments and dust and hairs onto the floor. Then she opened the box and lifted the two wax models—Junius's remaining ear and *her* ear—from their nest of gray silk. The replacement ear went on a stand in front of the mirror; the other one, next to it. She began—quite unnecessarily, since she'd finished carving it on Tuesday—comparing the mirrored ear with the other one. That little fold at the top of the helix. The angle was off about ten degrees. Of its own accord her hand reached for a small wax knife.

Why hadn't they shown up for the fitting? The impression taking last week had gone all right, a stoic Junius not even complaining, as most kids did, about the smell of the alginate or the creepy feel of it pouring over his skin. Eyes on the mirrored ear, Celia shaved minute curls of wax from the top, making it more Spock-like. Junius was one of her pro bono patients, referred by the children's unit at Shriners Burn Institute in Boston. A lot of people didn't like taking charity; maybe his redoubtable mama was one of them. When he finally did come in for the initial fitting, he'd be disappointed, of course. They all were, at first. It was too hard to imagine, when she held the colorless wax pretend ear to the ravaged opening, the lifelike eventual ear that would be there. Celia sometimes thought the most exhausting part of her work was the *convincing*. She had to do the imagining for both of them.

She was so absorbed that when her cell phone vibrated against her stomach—the strange not-quite-tickling sensation she always thought must be like feeling your unborn baby move—she jumped and dropped the wax knife. Her cell phone number was reserved for emergencies only. She took it out of her pocket and punched the "On" button.

Simon lay on the gurney under a stiff hospital sheet that left his feet bare. Corrugated plastic tubing, like a pastel vacuum-cleaner hose, protruded from his mouth and snaked its way to a monitor on a stand. Celia stood at Simon's head, the edge of the gurney pressing into her pelvis, and looked down. The ventilator's clear plastic mask flattened his beard and mustache; his face was alarmingly pale. As if in response to the sheer force of her attention, his eyelids began to flutter. *Open!* she said silently. But they didn't.

After some minutes, she pulled the stiff sheet over his feet, which, as her hand brushed them, felt like stone. Then she settled into the slippery vinyl visitor's chair to wait for Doctor Mikhailov. Folding her arms for warmth—why were hospitals always so cold?—she closed her eyes and let her ears fill with the rhythmic suck and sigh of the ventilator. When she opened them again, Simon's head was turned toward her and he was looking at her, his lips—or was it just the pressure of the plastic mask?—curved in the beginnings of a smile.

"*You* have got a *lovely* butt!"

Through the door, flung back so energetically it bounced off the bookcase next to it, came Junius in his chair. His mother, who was pushing it, was speaking over her shoulder to Edwin.

Relief—here they were, though without an appointment—flooded Celia. "Sit down, please," she said.

Edwin hovered. She'd never seen him blush before. She waved him away, and the door closed behind him. Mama parked the wheelchair alongside Celia's desk and settled her voluminous skirts—saffron silk, this time—into the visitor's chair. Her face beneath the broad brim of a fake leopard-skin hat wore a bright, expectant look. Maybe she'd mixed up the appointment times?

"I'm so sorry," Celia said. "I don't have the model—the ear—here in the office. We weren't expecting you. Can you come back tomorrow? Edwin will tell you what time." To Junius, she added, "I think you'll like it. It's going to look totally real."

Junius turned his head away and looked out the window.

"Junius! I don't know what's got into him, Doctor. Why, when we got on the bus he was so excited!"

Celia tried again. "You'll be able to put it on and take it off by yourself. Just snap and unsnap."

Without turning his head, Junius shrugged.

"It's very cool. Your buddies will be impressed."

Junius removed his gaze from the window and said, "He didn't stop. I'm gettin' down from the school bus, and I see this car coming, this blue van, and I see the driver lookin' at me, through the windshield. I *see* him."

"Simon'll be discharged soon," Leslie said.

They sat, Celia and Leslie, bundled in sweaters with quilts over their knees, in Leslie's dying garden. Joe had taken their son, Tommy, up to Boston, to the Museum of Science, where a special exhibit featured two hundred species of frogs, most of them deadly. The late morning sun was bright but cold. It gave Leslie's hair a dark crow's-wing shine. Leaves, faded to rose and ochre and brown, littered the flagstones and lay in drifts along the high cedar fence, and the nearly leafless maples threw an intricate net of shadows over the two women.

"You've been talking to my mother."

"Aunt Bess has nothing to do with it." Leslie's high-backed wooden chair creaked as she moved. She was incapable of talking without gestures. "But she did happen to mention that Simon's doctor thinks this time, when he leaves the ICU, he should go somewhere with round-the-clock care. Round-the-clock *nurses*. A nursing home, Seal."

She couldn't afford to get mad at Leslie. Without Leslie, she'd go under. "In the first place, I can take care of him. I *do* take care of him. In the second place, he'd never go."

"You're at work all day. He falls. Concussions, a hematoma, stitches. All those trips to the ER. He's the most pigheaded man I know. One of these days when he thinks he can manage—when he thinks, 'What am I, Professor Simon Feldstein, doing in a fucking wheelchair?'—he'll stand up and take off across the living room and break a hip. Then where'll you be? Where'll *he* be?"

Celia couldn't deny that it was a relief to drive homeward each evening in the deepening dusk with her husband in safe hands, no one waiting for her at the end of her journey. She picked up one of Tommy's action figures, which lay in a heap on the low wooden table between her and Leslie, and began bending its arms and legs into impossible positions. Always before, she'd been able to count on Leslie to understand that she couldn't send Simon away, not for his sake but for her own. That his presence, however diminished, was as necessary to her as breathing. Losing him, she would lose herself, Celia, the person she'd been all her adult life.

Leslie waved a hand. "If he insists on coming home, you could get East Bay Nursing to send somebody. They're good. We had them when Dad died. Then you could go up to Rogue Bluff and stay in the yurt. Get your bearings. Commute down here to your office a couple of days a week, or move the whole enchilada up there. I'll bet the VA and Shriners'd come to *you*. You're the best around."

Not so much best, as only. Most maxillofacial prosthetists went where the money was: either Hollywood or the CIA. Celia rolled the action figure between her palms. It was a superhero, she could tell from the cape and tights.

"Seal! Are you listening? Say Simon does insist on coming home. If you move out, he'll have to face how much he demands from you. How much help he needs now, to survive."

Celia thought, I should never have let her read Max's letter. Then she wouldn't know he offered me the yurt.

"Leslie—for God's sake! I couldn't just move out. You know I couldn't."

Leslie went on as if Celia hadn't spoken. "How many times have you told me, Maine lets you breathe. And Simon will be safe."

"Safety isn't the point. No one lives in order to be *safe*."

Leslie gathered up the manuscript pages she'd been working on when Celia arrived—she translated from Spanish and Portuguese, mostly legal and business documents, into English—and Tommy's Game Boy and assorted superheroes. "Let's go in. We can have tea. Peppermint, almond, or licorice? And there's some of Joe's *panettone*."

If even Leslie thought she should let go of Simon, then Celia had no allies at all. Despair washed through her. Her eyes moved over the wild, leaf-strewn margins of the garden, the yellowed stalks of what used to be snapdragons, the tall skeletons of hollyhocks and sunflowers. The sun was directly overhead now—it was almost noon—but she felt as cold as when they'd first sat down. "Fear no more the heat o' the sun," she murmured.

"What?"

"Shakespeare. It was the first thing Simon said when they took him off the ventilator yesterday. At least, it sounded like that was what he said."

Leslie rose, sloughing leaves off her lap. "Like some unknown nobody said: You can't prevent the birds of sorrow from flying over your head, but you can keep them from building a nest in your hair."

On warm nights Max liked to open the plastic skylight at the top of the yurt. Moonlight seemed to enter their bodies. The fragrance of the pines mingled with the smell of her own sweat and then with the scent they made together; the ringing of the crickets mixed with her own quick cries.

Afterwards, she lay with Max's body folded around hers and the sleeping bag folded around them both. Sometimes he snored, very lightly, a matter-of-fact sound, beautiful and ordinary. Sometimes the last thing she heard was the swift whisper of the zipper as he zipped them in, like the sound of a bird taking flight.

"I'll call you back this afternoon, Mom."

"What was it Simon used to say? When we die, God will reproach us for all the beauty He put on earth that we declined to enjoy."

"I've got a full waiting room out there. Simon never said any such thing."

"Thoreau, then. People need partners, Seal. We're mammals, after all."

"Drop it, Ma."

"If you fell in love, you'd feel better. All those endorphins. And don't call me Ma. You know perfectly well that no one would take me for your mother."

It had been August when he told her. More than eight years ago, now. For a week they'd been waiting, disbelief buttressing defiance, for the results of the MRI. It was a hot, somber, dark-skied afternoon. It was—

though she didn't realize this until years later—the very last time his
illness was the same experience for both of them. She bit her lip hard,
blood salty on her tongue, so as not to cry. They made love, not desper-
ately (that would come later), not despairingly (that would come later
still), but determinedly. Like two people trying to say everything—past,
future, *now*—in a single telegram.

Afterwards, they lay with their cooling bodies tight together, their
heads on the same pillow. She turned her face away so that he wouldn't
taste her tears. Her hair, long then, tugged painfully against her scalp
where his head held it fast to the pillow. A hot breeze sifted through
the open window, and they could hear the far-off rumbling of a slowly
approaching thunderstorm.

"Everything that grows," he'd whispered into her hair, in his Shakespeare voice, "holds in perfection but a little moment."

"A yurt—that's some kind of tent, right? Are you crazy?"

"You've been talking to Leslie. That's *her* idea. It's just an idea."

"All alone in the *woods*?"

"Mom. I have to hang up now. I haven't seen Simon yet today."

"You could stay here, in the spare room. Even Thoreau went
home once a week. Did you know that? He took his laundry home to
his mother."

Celia settled in her chair and looked down at the day's roster. Henry
Threadgill, referred from Shriners Burn Institute—F, 24, B—for the
third time this year ("Nose itch—a bitch," Edwin had written next
to his name); Amar Singh, the beautiful young man from Bombay,
whose dark-blue turban hid the ear misshapen since birth; Mrs. de
Carvalho. But where was Junius? Celia's stomach gave a little leap,
anticipating the moment when she would snap his new ear into

place. Anticipating the sight of his face looking sideways into the mirror she'd hold up to him.

She buzzed Edwin.

The intercom crackled. "Yeah?"

"Junius Johns. He's coming back today for his fitting. What time?"

"They cancelled. There was a message from big mama on the voicemail this morning. I put old Threadgill in their spot."

Relax. Breathe.

Celia undid the waistband button on her good gray pants, breathed deeper, and looked out the window, blinking back tears. Outside, it was a perfect day. Burning blue sky; the last deep-red leaves twirling down from the Japanese maple, released; the sun coming in at a golden slant through its polished branches.

What was it the nuns had taught them, in Saturday catechism class? They'd had to chant it, a dozen seven-year-old voices piping in unison, hands clapping the beat. The SINS against HOPE are PRESUMPTION and DESPAIR. Why would Junius blow her off? They'd had a rapport. He'd spoken. Even his mother had been amazed. Why would she not bring him back?

But maybe that *was* why. That's what Simon would say. The Theory of Paradoxical Causality, he used to call it. The very reason people should do something was often the reason they didn't.

The thing was, she could not imagine it: the hopeful sound of zippers, the shuffle of luggage down the ramp into the driveway, the wheelchair in the doorway jerking around, presenting her with Simon's eloquent back. Couldn't imagine looking, one day not long from now, out her office window at her loaded pickup, its blue tarp dusted with the season's first snow. Couldn't imagine driving, at the end of the afternoon's work, not west, but north.

Romantic Fever ❀

SHE'S HAD THE DREAM AGAIN. THE DREAM SHE CAN NEVER REMEMBER once she wakes up, that leaves behind only its vinegar taste, its coating of sweat. Her heart is going like a gerbil in a gerbil wheel. The swell of her own breathing fills her ears, and the damp sheets pin her arms at her sides like a mummy.

She moves her hand, an inch at a time, until she feels Blankie. Her fingers catch in it and wind it tight, its hairy thickness, the cool silk of its binding. She mustn't fall asleep again. What if she never wakes up? Since the romantic fever, she has to be careful all the time. *Rheumatic* fever. She was so sick she missed her First Communion with the rest of the second grade in the spring, so sick she almost died. She heard the doctor tell her mother out in the hospital corridor when they thought she was asleep. It was right before President Kennedy got shot to death. Her mother says if she isn't careful, she'll get sick again. Her heart is *fragile*: like the gilded china swan on the mantel in the living room.

Afraid to open her eyes, she lies wrapped in the still heat. What if there's nothing out there, only darkness pressing down like the lid of a mummy's box? What if there's no one? Then she hears her mother and Bob starting up to bed. Their voices rise and fall: the sound of arguing.

"Mother of God, how can I?"

"Mother—that's just it. Mother her less, Jeanie."

"I have to keep her safe. You don't know what it's like—"

"Yeah, yeah, yeah. Mothers! Who's holding the world *up*? Who keeps the plane in the air when you fly?"

They're in the hallway now. Bob used to make her mother laugh a lot; sometimes she'd hear them laughing in bed at night. This isn't a real, true joke, though. She knows Bob's joke voice.

"If you could just . . ." The bedroom door shuts on her mother's words, on the tight note in her mother's voice.

She opens her eyes. A little light sifts through the blinds from the streetlamp outside her window. Slowly the darkness gathers and clots into familiar shapes: the swinging rattan chair that hangs from a hook Bob put in the ceiling, the dresser, the shelf of stuffed animals. She's thirsty—since the drought started, she feels thirsty all the time—but she's afraid to get out of bed. Her head hurts where the lumps of her braids press into it. After her hair wash on Saturday nights, her mother braids it wet, the way she does for customers at Hair and Now. When she gets dressed for Mass in the morning, her hair will ripple down her back almost to her waist.

Out in the dark, a distant train rattles past, trailing the long streamers of its whistle. On Monday Bob will take the train down to San Diego for his cousin's wedding. A hundred miles. The best man. Sleepy now, she sees him swept up in the train's thunder and pulled away, growing smaller and smaller, into the dark. Who is safe? Presidents get shot to death. She could get the fever again—could even die. Her *mother* could die. If her mother died, would Bob go away for good?

But the thought flies off. Sleep sucks at her, pulling her down, folding her tight.

Kneeling, she leans her elbows on the pew in front and buries her face in her hands, even though she hasn't been to Communion. Fans push

the smell of women's perfume back and forth, and ruffle the damp
bangs that fall over her fingers. Usually when it's this hot somebody
faints—one of the fragrant, bare-armed women in ice-cream colors,
pink and white and pale green, or one of the girls in stiff organdy
dresses like hers. Not today. Maybe it's the tension. The fire watch has
been on for a whole week now. They can't run under the sprinkler or
have a barbecue or fireworks. It's as bad as the fever. Can't do this, can't
do that. Be *careful*.

Here is the church; here is the steeple. She looks around her through
laced fingers. Beside her, Tommy, who's been to Communion, rests
his forehead on his folded hands. His sandy hair sticks up in little spikes,
and his plaid cowboy shirt has dark patches on it. He doesn't kneel up
straight but slumps with his behind on the seat like the men do, though
he's only two years older than she is. On her other side, Bob isn't kneeling at all; he sits on the edge of the pew. To see his face she has to look
way up out of the corner of her eye. His skin is tan, with white lines like
rays around his eyes. He's leafing through the hymnbook, sometimes
stopping to read one of the hymns. The thick black book looks small
in his hands. There's gray-green dirt under his fingernails and around
the cuticles, metal dust from his job at the plant. She lifts her face and
turns her fingers, still clasped, inside out. *Open the door and see all the
people*. Beyond Bob is her mother, in her silky dress the orange-yellow
color of her hair, kneeling straight as a school pencil. She can't go to
Communion because of not being married to Bob. Tommy, her, Bob,
Mom. Anyone would think they were a real family, son and daughter,
father and mother, like the one in the poster next to the blackboard at
school. "The Family That Prays Together Stays Together."

But they don't, really. Pray together. Bob hasn't been to Communion, either; he never goes, because he isn't Catholic. She can't
remember what he is—maybe nothing? Before she got the fever, she'd
almost finished the second grade catechism, getting ready to make her

First Communion. So she knows: if Bob hasn't been baptized, then when he dies he can't go to Heaven. Unbaptized souls go to Limbo, Sister Marie Kathleen told them, out of sight of the Divine Presence, because souls with the stain of Original Sin aren't allowed to see God. She pictures the soul: like her mother's dressmaker's dummy that stands in the attic—armless, legless, headless—except it's made of gold. A golden bodice fitting neatly just under the skin. When you're baptized, it's engraved with a seal, imprinted, stamped forever: OKAY FOR HEAVEN.

Bob's soul will go to Limbo and wait forever in that place. In the dark. Alone. Just thinking of it, she starts to feel the night fears tickling, crawling over her. Choking; airless; a dry, parched place. She remembers the pictures in the *Young Catholic Messenger*, the black silhouettes of Communists saying, "We Will Bury You." Her breath comes in short wet puffs into her palms. Can't breathe. Can't move. Rusty scream of iron hinges, door thudding shut. *She* is the mummy.

She gulps in air. Bob is looking down at her. "Do you feel faint, honeybunch?" he says. He looks at her closely; then his face smoothes out and he reaches over to tickle her gently in the ribs. "Don't!" she whispers. A fat ice-cream-colored woman in the pew in front turns to stare. Bob folds his hands and looks solemn, then crosses his eyes.

If only Bob and her mother would get married! But they won't. Her mother explained the whole thing a year ago, sitting close between her and Tommy on the sofa in her furry bathrobe the night before Bob moved in, using a lot of words they didn't know: *liberated, commitment, stereotype*. "Modern times, chickies," she said. "No wedding's gonna change anything. No piece of paper. Rituals don't make people stay together."

If Bob got baptized, though. Yes! Then even if he left them, like their father did when she was a baby, even if he died, they'd be able to find him again. In Heaven.

Tommy's elbow digs into her shoulder. Everyone is standing for the final hymn. When she stands up, her mother reaches around Bob to touch her hair, smoothing it back over her shoulders, casually brushing a hand along her cheek to see if she's feverish. She shrugs out of reach. Voices swell around her, a hollow sound like a seashell held to her ear. *I once was lost, bu-ut now am found. Was blind, bu-uh-ut now I see. A-MAZing grace . . .* She pictures grace: a silvery rain, like tinsel, falling straight down onto the poor scuffed soul. When you're baptized, you get a shower of grace that washes off Original Sin, the way her mother sluices water over food scraps in the sink.

Ho-ow sweet the sound. They file out of the pew and Bob genuflects on his left knee, the way he always does. "One knee is as good as the other," he said once, when her mother tried to instruct him. His broad back, white-shirted, fills her vision, blocking out the families shuffling slowly up the aisle ahead of them. Her mother links her arm through Bob's and smiles up at him, then looks straight ahead. Tommy pulls his shirt out and flaps it to stir the air. Exactly noon, and the sound of the steeple bells drops through the haze of organ music like grace, and the four of them walk through the carved wooden doors and out under the live oak that spreads its branches between them and the sky.

While her mother makes Sunday dinner, she's supposed to take a nap. This is because of the romantic fever. She waits for the clang of pots and pans from the kitchen, then slides out of bed to go find Tommy. Usually they spend her naptime out back with the rabbits. Today she really needs to talk to him—to unfold her plan. First, though, she'll have to make him see the problem.

She takes Blankie for company down the empty hall, the long, silent stairway. Passing her mother's room, she pauses. She never comes in here except once in a while in the middle of the night, if the dream is bad enough. The room breathes her mother's perfume. Sheer curtains printed with blue cabbage roses belly in the breeze. Bob's suitcase lies open on the bed.

She steps over the threshold and walks in. So far the brown leather bag holds only underwear. She fingers the mysterious ribby texture, the tough elastic. What if Bob never comes back? The thought makes her feel cold all over, and she hugs Blankie tight to her chest. She stands there, not thinking exactly, more like waiting. Then she shakes out Blankie and folds it carefully into a square and tucks it into the side pocket of the suitcase.

"That's *dumb*." Tommy is standing in the doorway.

"So?" A little corner of plaid wool is sticking up out of the pocket. She pats it into place.

"So come on!" Tommy says. "Let's go."

Outside, the sky is almost white. They pad single file down the hill behind the house, through long grass lying bleached and limp. Heat rises around them, and there's a faint smoky taste in the air. They move like Indians, sure-footed and silent.

At the bottom of the yard the rabbit hutch stands on a platform Bob built. He set it on six-by-sixes buried so deep in the ground even a golden retriever wouldn't be able to knock it over. The hutch, made of heavy twisted wire, is divided into two compartments. Lopka, the mother, is in the left-hand one with her babies, and Jack, the father, is in the other. "This is Jack Bunny," Bob said the day he brought the two rabbits home. "And this is his wife." One was brown, one gray and white, with long ears that hung down. He carried them right into the bedroom and sat down on the edge of the bed and put them into her arms. Still weak from the fever, she held them awkwardly, one in each arm, and rubbed her chin along their backs. They were small then, only eight weeks old.

She checks on the three babies first. They spent their first two weeks inside the nesting box, invisible unless she parted the mound of hay and torn-out fur to look for them. Now, eyes still sealed shut, they bumble around like Mr. Magoo. She opens Lopka's door and reaches into the nesting box. She scoops up one of the gray-and-white babies and hands it to Tommy; the brown one she holds herself. She cradles it in the crook of one arm, supporting its back legs the way Bob showed her. It's warm and soft, but it squirms, and its nails dig into her bare arm like tiny needles. She tightens her arms around it. Yesterday its eyelids began to part; now they're narrow slits holding a faint black glitter.

"Listen," she says. "Bob isn't baptized, right?"

"Yeah," Tommy says, not looking up from his rabbit. "So?"

"So." The brown baby gives a little leap in her arms. "If he dies, we wouldn't ever see him again."

A fly buzzes in the stillness, and Jack moves restlessly in his cage.

"He's lonely," she says. "He wants to be in the same cage with Lopka and the babies."

"Naw. He doesn't care. He's probably just hungry."

Turning away, she lays her cheek against the baby rabbit's soft back.

"He wouldn't *burn*," Tommy says. "He wouldn't go to Hell, or even Purgatory. Just Limbo. There's no fire there."

"He'd miss us. He'd be lonely. We need to baptize him, Tom. We need to do it right away."

Tommy looks unconvinced. He doesn't understand, because he doesn't know what she knows. Sometimes now, since the fever, she feels older than he is, older than Bob and her mother, older than *anybody*.

She says, "He could leave. He isn't married to Mom. He could leave anytime."

Tommy tightens his grip on the baby rabbit, which squirms in protest. "Like Dad did." His freckles stand out in his white face.

In her arms the brown baby begins to tremble. It tosses its head over and over, and its long ears slide flat against its head. She can see its eyelids quiver. The black glitter between them widens, and then, slowly, the lids pull apart. "Tommy. Look!" The shadow of her own head and shoulders falls across the baby rabbit, and she imagines how she fills the circle of its vision. She—*she*—is the first thing it's ever seen. Its eyes are dark purple like plums. How could the eyes be the windows of the soul, the way Sister Marie Kathleen said? You couldn't ever see down that far, through the tangled veins, the branches of bone.

Tommy says, "We'd have to sneak up on him."

She looks up from the brown rabbit, which is struggling in her arms now, blinking, its head turning back and forth. The color has come back into Tommy's face. "In his sleep," she says, "we could do it in his sleep," and waits.

"After dinner." Tommy fills in the rest of her plan as if he'd thought of it himself. "When he takes his nap."

They put the babies back and watch the brown one leap across the hutch floor to Lopka. Before they leave, they fill the water bottles from the bucket underneath the platform and put extra hay in both feeders. *A-maz-ing grace*, she hums to herself as they make their way back up the hill. A-MAZ-*ing*, MAZ*ing*. But a thin snake of fear has crawled into her stomach and lies there in a knot. Once they can see, the babies will start to run around, they'll get into things. They'll be much harder to keep safe.

In the kitchen Bob keeps the radio on during dinner. Her mother wants to get a television set, maybe even color, but Bob says no.

Her mother dishes out cold chicken and sliced tomatoes and three-bean salad and shuffles the plates across the plastic lace cloth, one, two, three, four. Then, with a sigh, she sits down and fluffs out her hair.

"Everybody set?"

They listen to the news. The pope is sick. (Her mother frowns anxiously.) The governor is having a birthday party in Sacramento. (Bob snorts.) Fire has broken out in the San Gabriel Mountains; they're digging firebreaks to the north and east of L.A.; rain is expected later today.

She bends over her plate. Half an hour for dinner; half an hour to clean up after. Then her mother will go upstairs to finish packing Bob's suitcase, and Bob will listen to the ball game and fall sleep. The plastic seat of her chair sticks wetly to her bare legs; when she moves, it makes a sucking sound. Bob talks about the weather; her mother doesn't answer, but she can see her sneaking looks at him. This is how they act when they fight. It feels as if the room, the house, is holding its breath.

"I'm thirsty," she says.

Bob gets up and goes to the refrigerator and comes back with a pewter pitcher of iced tea. She reaches for it. Cold but sweaty, it's so heavy her wrist bends as she lifts it.

"Chickie! Be care—" Her mother bites her lip and looks at Bob. He frowns back. The pitcher's fat curved handle starts to slide. She grabs it with both hands. Her wrists feel as if they're going to snap. The pitcher wavers and ice cubes thud into her glass, splashing her hands with cold tea. Heart racketing in her chest, she sets the pitcher down. When she looks up, Bob is smiling at her.

From the screened porch comes the announcer's voice, the sound of the crowd. She can see the back of Bob's head as he lies in the recliner, his arm down by the side of the chair. The way his hand dangles along the floorboards says he's already asleep.

Tommy goes into the front hall and comes back wearing the

Dodgers cap Bob got him. Once Tommy is with you, he doesn't hold back. He puts his lips to her ear. "I can't find my missal," he whispers. "We'll have to fake it."

Carrying the bowl of water in both hands, she starts for the porch, but Tommy's hand shoots out to grab her wrist. "Indians!" They cross the porch as stealthily as if they were approaching a bird in the grass. Bob's eyes are closed; his belly, sloping gently in his undershirt, rises and falls. His bare feet, stuck out in front of him on the recliner, are white, with long knotted toes like roots. Beside him the radio buzzes and snaps.

Tommy looks at the bowl. Sweat glitters across his nose and cheeks. *Okay*, he mouths. He points to her, then to the other side of the chair. Assuming a scornful expression to let him know he's not really taking over, she moves around to Bob's other side. From between his parted lips the breath emerges in little zipper sounds.

The radio farts, a loud pop. "It's . . . a . . . base hit!" the announcer says.

Bob stirs and groans. She jumps back behind his chair. In the bowl between her hands, the water sloshes dangerously. She freezes; Tommy does, too. Rigid, they wait. The sisal matting bites into the bottoms of her bare feet. She hears a far-off sound: thunder, from the other side of the valley. Through the screens, clouds have begun massing in the sky behind the rabbit hutch, stone-colored and heavy-looking.

When Bob starts snoring again, she moves back to her place beside him. Tommy gives the visor of his cap a quick tug. *Ready?* She sets the bowl down on the floor. She cups her left hand and dips up water. Rising, she nods. *Go.*

Tommy's lips move. So low she can barely hear him, he murmurs, "Do you renounce Satan and all his works? And all his . . . his pomps? Then I baptize thee in the name of the Father. And of the Son. And of the Holy Ghost."

"Till death do us part," she whispers, keeping her cupped fingers tight together.

Tommy crosses himself. "Amen."

She slides the fingers of her right hand into the water she holds in her left. A wild, pale light the color of grace pours in through the screens and washes over Bob's face. She raises her hand high above him, above the spot where the dome of his chest conceals the golden bodice. A few drops fall like little gray dimes onto his undershirt. His eyelids flicker. Bending down close so that she will be the first thing he sees, she shakes her hand, and over them both a thousand drops sparkle and fall.

Autumn, 1911 ❀

HUMOR CRAWLED AT THE CORNERS OF HER MOUTH, AND HER NOSE was wet: those were the things I noticed first about Sophie.

She came to live in our house at the beginning of October, in 1911, a month after my thirteenth birthday. My mother and Sophie were first cousins, close in girlhood but long separated by their respective marriages—one disastrous, one lustrous.

"Oh, Alice! *Alice*," was all Sophie said before my mother's arms went round her. Mama had to duck beneath her cousin's wide-brimmed, flower-laden hat. Late afternoon light, flooding through the etched glass of our broad front door into the vestibule where we stood, poured over the two women. Their bodies, the same height but far from the same girth, made me think of Mary meeting Saint Anne in the stained-glass window above the side altar at Holy Name. When they drew apart, my father was still standing to one side, derby in hand, regarding them with a fondness that seemed somehow equally distributed. The two women stood with fingers lightly linked. They were the same age, thirty-four, but Sophie was fat—not plump, but fat—in the way the ripe Alberta peaches in my mother's garden were fat. It made her a blurred copy of my beautiful mother. Mama was laughing softly, for no reason, for sheer joy. The white of her shirtwaist glowed in the mellow light; her bosom (which for a year or so I had been trying not to look at, or at least not to be seen looking at) moved up and down with her laughter.

"Charles!" Papa motioned to me to step forward. "Shake hands with your cousin," and I did. Papa said, "Leave your mantle with your valise, Sophia. Effie or George will see to them. Alice, my dear, shall we have tea?"

My mother, pink with embarrassment because these suggestions should have come from her, took the coat—one of the voluminous garments called "dusters" meant for riding in the new horseless carriages—out of Sophie's hands and laid it across her large ostrich-skin bag. Sophie unpinned her hat and Mama set it on the hall table. Then she led the way through the carved double doors into the parlor.

Over tea in front of the big fieldstone fireplace, the grown-ups talked of things that did not interest me. From my corner I watched them, seated around the fire—built high despite the warmth of the October day just ending—three points in an isosceles triangle. Between the grown-ups' remarks there was quiet in the room except for the snap of the fire in the grate, the occasional passing of a carriage in the street outside. Effie had not yet lit the lamps. Allotted one cup of grassy-tasting China tea, I drank and watched dusk accumulate in the corners of the room.

Papa shook out the evening paper and ran his eyes down the front page. "The Turks are at it again," he observed, stroking his mustache. He had more than one vanity, but the greatest of them was his dark, abundant mustache. "Cholera. Censorship. And they've expelled all the Italians."

"Poor souls!" Mama said. "All those families made to leave their homes."

"Taft claims he's got the railroads under control . . . Trusts now curbed . . . Researchers find beer keeps best in brown bottles . . . Mrs. Taft to go to hot springs for health. Ah, yes," said Papa, folding the paper and flinging it onto the carpet by his feet. "Maybe they'll feed her beer in brown bottles."

Sophie laughed. Her nose, still wet at the tip, caught the firelight. She gleamed all over: her wide face, her hands, plump and ringless, her arms in tight silk sleeves the color of blackberries resting on the carved arms of her chair. For some reason I remembered at that moment that silk was spun from the saliva of silkworms: my cousin wore a dress of spit.

A silence; then, "'Here we will sit and let the sounds of music / Creep in our ears,'" Mama said. My mother muttered poetry the way other people hummed tunes, unaware, in snatches. When she was happy, it was Shakespeare; when she was sad, Keats; if she was terribly worried, she threw off bits of Dante's *Inferno*.

"It's what music would look like," Sophie said, staring into the flames. "Fire. It's the sound of trumpets."

Papa said nothing, only stroked his mustache. He stretched out his long legs—he was six foot four and slender, a graceful giraffe of a man—and crossed one elegantly shod foot over the other. A position he would only take *en famille*. But then, Sophie *was* family.

It's so hard to know, at the time, what to treasure. Now, so long afterwards, that first evening seems a template for all that followed. For the whole extended, languorous, breath-held autumn of 1911, the last we were to spend as a family. If (as Papa, smiling his gently cynical smile, would have said) human beings can learn from experience, wouldn't I know what it is I should be cherishing now, in 1971?

Looking back, I see three grown-ups seated companionably around the fire, separate but connected. And I? I am sitting on a hassock off to one side. Instinctively I've taken the position of observer, and so I will remain. *Voyeur*—a word from the French novels I am not supposed to know the hiding place of. Simply what, not quite having left childhood, I have always been?

The morning star was still faintly visible from my bedroom window when Papa left the next day, as usual, for the factory. I watched him walk briskly down the wide semi-circular driveway, derby hat at its usual raffish angle, coat collar upturned against the chill morning air. The big iron gates clanged behind him. I could still hear the decisive sound of his steps on the cobblestones after he'd vanished into the street. My room faced east; I sat for a while watching the sky stain a deeper and deeper rose. It was in these moments at dawn that I felt closest to my father—not to *him*, but to the essence of him, the visceral, almost-breathing link between him and the factory he had made out of nothing.

"Rope, Charlie! Rope! *Ça va sans dire*. Virtually no one," my father often declared, "understands the importance of rope." Think, he would exhort me (or Mama, or Effie, or even my friends), of all the things that could not exist without it. Block and tackle, tents, elevators, grandfather clocks, hot-air balloons, military uniforms, bridges, hammocks, toboggans, boxing rings—the list went on and on. Think of all the things we would not be able to do: brand cattle, climb mountains, ride a Ferris wheel, throw a life preserver to someone drowning.

And the best, the strongest, the most trustworthy rope made? Oiseau's, of course. If everyone did not know that, they should; because every time they rode in those elevators, crossed those bridges, stepped into one of those hot-air balloons, they entrusted their lives to rope. The crates in which my father's rope was shipped bore the legend:

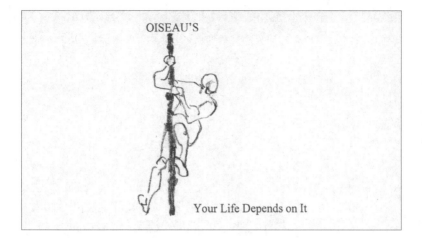

OISEAU'S

Your Life Depends on It

On the day I turned seven—the age, according to Holy Mother Church, of reason—my father had taken me into his study and set me on his big leather chair. He sat on the edge of the glass-topped mahogany desk, swinging his long thin legs, and told me a story.

Before he became the husband of Alice, the father of me, Francis Xavier Oiseau had belonged, for nearly two decades, to no one. His parents were killed in a boating accident in 1877, when he was nine years old. In Quebec, where he'd lived all his life up till then, a steamboat boiler exploded in midafternoon of a windless gray day on the St. Lawrence River. Most of the two hundred passengers were killed: burned, blown to pieces, drowned. *Un horreur, ça, un horreur que dure toute la vie.* Clinging to his life preserver, the boy Francis saw his mother's body float by, face down and sinking in the turbulent, scalding water. His two small sisters clung to her bloody skirts.

My mother burst into the room through the French doors. "For God's sake, Francis! What's possessed you?" She was very angry, red-faced, shouting, her hair askew from working in the garden—exactly the way my elegant father liked her least. They were still arguing that night, after I'd been put to bed. I heard my mother's voice as they ascended the stairs. ". . . your benighted Church!" She'd been raised Congregationalist and had only converted to Catholicism in order to marry my father. Papa's reply was indistinct; Mama got louder. ". . . reason descends on everyone at the same age? And at *that* age? Obviously it failed to descend on *them!*"

Now the sound of dogs barking, at first distant, then louder, flowed down the street toward my open window. The lamplighter paused outside our gate and raised his pole to extinguish the gaslight there. I became aware of the house awakening: the far-off clang of the stove's iron lids, Effie on the back stairs, singing (*He took her by the lily-white hand*), the slap of the morning-room shutters briskly folded back. Then the sun burst through the honey locusts by the high stone wall where our driveway ended.

It must have been a hot, sunny day, that day in my father's study. I can still recall the smell of dust and library paste (which tasted—I had verified this some months before—exactly like it smelled) and the sound of a trapped fly assaulting the windows. My father's father's body was never found. There were no other relatives; he and his sisters were brought to a Catholic orphanage. Nine years after that, the Canadian light infantry took young Francis and sent him to Khartoum. Discharged in the spring of 1890, he came to Providence to visit a former comrade-in-arms, and stayed. With the army pay he'd saved, and a loan from the comrade, he started Oiseau's.

Nowadays a child of seven would never be told the story of my grandparents' death. The Age of Reason—no one even uses the phrase anymore. Perhaps my mother was right? Looking back from what most would call a venerable age, I do not think so. Looking back, I see the sunlit plain of childhood with its view in all directions, pure and clear as mathematics; and then the occluding cloud of puberty—of unexpected hair and traitorous voice and swelling and yearning—of unreason, descends.

I escaped into the burning autumn afternoon with Brother Aloysius's bell ringing behind me. "First one out, are ye then, Charles?" he shouted, as he did every afternoon, hauling on the rope while the bell above him flung its recurring shadow across his round red face. He had to turn around in order for his words to follow me—I was that fast. In the five weeks since school started I'd already established myself as the best sprinter at Holy Name Academy.

The Dugout, as I called it, was my destination. On the western edge of town, it was carved into a hillside beneath a profusion of wild grape, its opening further hidden by an old wooden door onto which I'd glued masses of brambles. Between the road—rutted and little traveled—and the Dugout was an old, abandoned orchard. Unharvested apples lay in the long grass, giving off a rich, haunting smell of decay. Bees puttered ceaselessly among them. Their collective hum rising around me seemed to draw me in—to separate me from the world of carriages and pocket watches and factories.

I shifted the heavy door; brambles clawed my hands. I pulled aside the piece of cheesecloth (stolen from Effie's cleaning closet) that served as a curtain to keep out bees, and threw myself down. The Dugout's packed dirt floor—it had hardly rained all that autumn—felt cool through my woolen school uniform. The space, a natural grotto I'd gradually enlarged over the two previous summers, was five feet wide and six feet deep. If I stood up, my head hit packed earth held in place by roots and rocks. On this warm October afternoon I lay on my stomach in the pleasant, chilly gloom with my weight on my elbows and my chin on my palms and breathed in the odors of earth and rotting apples. Outside, two cardinals called from tree to tree. I could tell their sex by their calls. The female cardinal has two: a brief, inquiring one that sounds like "Where are you?" and a longer, fancier one, "Oh! *There* you are!" The male has only a single soaring cry: "I'm here! I'm here!" Over and over this female called, and the male responded. There would be a few minutes' pause. Then she'd begin to ask again.

Was this how it was supposed to be between the sexes?

I'd gone through the whole eight years of grammar school with Cordelia Huddle. In fifth grade we'd shared a double desk. By the end of that year, in which we discovered a mutual passion for books purloined from our parents (holding them on our laps beneath the broad wooden desk top and turning the pages stealthily), we were best friends. Secret friends. It was, we knew, a toss-up which of our classmates would have been more contemptuous, the boys or the girls. This year, the first year of high school, we were both at Holy Name. For me this meant long pants, a book bag instead of a leather strap, and moving from room to room down dim polished corridors. The girls' half was completely separate; there was one connecting door, at the end of the second-floor corridor, and that was kept locked.

It wasn't the way it used to be, between me and Cordelia. Or rather, it was, and then suddenly it wasn't, and then it was again. We met nearly every day a half-hour or so before school started. Papa's early departure for the factory woke me, and Cordelia got up before anyone else in her house. She slept with a long string tied to her wrist which she let down the wall outside her bedroom window, and the lamplighter tugged on it when he passed by. We'd be sitting on the chill stone of the Academy wall, sitting and talking, the way we'd always talked, about a book we were reading or the latest secret code one of us had discovered (we were crazy about cryptography) or the unfathomable idiocies of grown-ups. Carriages would begin to rattle over the cobblestones, and the milkman would come clinking down the street and cry, "Morning, you two!" Then suddenly, in mid-sentence, there would come this sense of intrusion. As if a stranger had sat down between us. Cordelia felt it, too. I could tell by the way her eyes slid away from mine and her hands clasped each other, long fingers with their bitten nails gripping tight.

I turned over onto my back and lay looking up at the packed dirt and roots of the Dugout's ceiling. The smell of the earth on which I lay, of the long grass beyond the cheesecloth curtain, dry and sweet, of apples decomposing—these blended and seemed to enclose me in a single scent not vegetable at all. Without my willing it, I felt my penis rise, my buttocks tighten. One hand unbuttoned the fly of my trousers. The other, of its own accord, closed around the shaft. It began to slide up and down, the wrist tickled by the soft new hair. I heard a cardinal's call again. Only the male, my mind noted, while my hand moved faster. *I'm here! I'm here!* Over and over he called, unanswered. Over and over. Faster and faster. *I'm here! I'm here!* Until I found myself at the edge of the realm I'd discovered years before and then for years forgotten, the place I called Quette. The place of warmth and soaring light and peace.

Entering the orchard was like coming home to myself. I called it the Dugout after the ones settlers made to live in on the Kansas prairie; "fort" was childish, and "foxhole" had yet to be invented, along with all the other horrors of the Great War.

A pair of legs in black-and-white-striped stockings swung back and forth at the level of my head. The crossed feet, shoeless, arched and nuzzled each other like small plump animals.

"Cousin Sophie?" What an idiot I must have sounded! Who else could such limbs have belonged to?

"Charlie!" She sounded pleased to see me.

She was perched on the scaffolding above the door I'd just opened. If I hadn't jumped back, she would have kicked me. She sat facing away from the door. I ducked under the swinging legs and walked into the middle of the room. "Room" isn't the right word. There was a floor of polished slate, but the walls were no more than a semicircle of iron arches open to the October morning, and above my head the intense blue sky was divided into triangles by the iron frame of what would eventually be a large glass dome. Sunlight glinted off metal where the dew had not yet dried. Dazzled, I looked away.

Sophie lifted one of Effie's rhubarb tarts to her mouth and her small white teeth sank into the crust. Something about the way her full lips pressed together as she chewed made me want a rhubarb tart more than anything in the world. She threw back her head. Her hair floated out around her in the quickening air. It was the first time I'd seen it loose, though she'd been living with us now for nearly two weeks. Crinkled, like the crystal pleats of my mother's best shirtwaist, it fell nearly to her waist, and in the sun its unremarkable dark blonde became a rainbow as she moved. I tried not to stare.

"Isn't it a beautiful, beautiful morning?" she cried, her mouth still full. Bits of rhubarb pulp arced into the sunshine; one struck me on the cheek and stuck there. It would have been impolite to wipe it away.

"How did you get up there?" I asked.

Sophie pointed behind me. I turned. Around the perimeter of the orangerie was scaffolding as high as my head, with—at the far end of the room to be—pegs hammered into one of the posts. "You *climbed* up?" My voice, always treacherous now, gave a mouse-like squeak on "up." "You walked those planks?"

"'Course!" Sophie crammed the rest of the tart into her mouth and chewed. I tried to imagine her skipping around the room on a foot-wide plank. For reasons I couldn't articulate, it felt wrong for her to be here, in this place that was my mother's, so long imagined by her and only just beginning its existence. It was as if Sophie had invaded my mother's dreams.

The plump striped legs resumed swinging. Sophie's long yellow skirt flew up and down, revealing a froth of petticoat that made my heart stammer. In the fashion of the day, her wide breasts were covered yet somehow *offered*. Try as I might to keep my eyes away from legs, froth, breasts, I could feel my face grow hot. The dome's iron skeleton cast a net of shadows over the two of us, and the morning noises of birds, like an orchestra tuning up, filled the air with possibility.

During our exchange a far-off honking had drawn nearer. Now a flock of Canada geese passed above our heads. Their formation, wavering but purposeful, traced a dark V. The sky above them looked as if it might burst; below them, blood-bright maples—the ones that would shade the unfinished dome in future summers—burned.

"Isn't it *glorious?*" cried Sophie. "I can't see why in the world Alice wants to wall this in. She ought to make a terrace here, a big open space. Not a conservatory."

"Orangerie," I corrected. The rush of her feet, back and forth, past my head stirred up the smells of the place—cold iron, fresh-sawn wood—and Sophie's own smell, like summer grass. The combination went to my head like a few sips of port at Christmas. Feeling disloyal, I tried to push away this pleasant dizziness. "It's Mama's lifelong dream," I said. "To have an orangerie. My father has given it to her for their wedding anniversary, their fifteenth." Inexplicably, a sappy phrase I would ordinarily have died rather than use leapt out of my mouth. "He loves her dearly."

Sophie looked up into the bright sky. "You're a tad pompous, aren't you?" she said. Then, "Look!"

"What?" But as I spoke, I saw it.

A bird had flown into the space beneath the dome. It darted from one side to the other, more and more agitated—as if the glass had already been installed, as if it were truly trapped.

Sophie cried, "Oh, Charlie! *Do* something!"

Her voice made me feel suddenly taller. I ran across the floor and clambered up the ladder of pegs. Sweat from my hands made them slippery. Up on the scaffolding—narrower under my feet than it had seemed from below—I felt as if the blue sky were pulling me into itself. The bird, by now a concentrated ball of terror, was dashing itself against the broad iron frame of the dome, bouncing from point to point along the circle, freedom inches above its head. The scaffolding made a square just inside the circle of the dome. I stood on one side of the square; Sophie sat in the middle of the adjoining side. Midway between us was the bird. It was a sparrow—brown with a black bib.

I edged closer. The pine plank shifted beneath the leather soles of my boots. The sound whenever the bird hit the iron was surprisingly loud. *Thump. Thump.* Moving slowly towards it, I felt the impact in my own chest. I didn't dare look down. When I got level with the sparrow, I stopped. Now what? There was a good six feet between the scaffolding I stood on and the iron frame against which the bird continued to hurl itself. I imagined a lariat, like the ones cowboys used. Putting one hand on a joist for balance, I started unbuttoning my suspenders with the other.

"Be careful!" Sophie said.

I left the right front button for last, so that I could grab one end of the suspenders as they fell. I looked down. The slate floor seemed far away. The bird came to rest on a sort of ledge where the dome's base rested on a massive iron column. It sat, quivering, at the level of my eyes and about six feet away. I could see the bright black shoe-button of its eye. We were two creatures equally afraid.

I flung my arm wide, swinging the suspenders out and up. The motion pulled me off balance. I grabbed the joist. The end of my make-shift lariat missed the bird but drove it upward. It hung there—in the open sky. I could see its scaly feet clutch at empty air. Now! I thought, and let go of the joist. Balancing on the very edge of the beam, I threw my suspenders at the bird. It flew upward, flapping its wings in quick bursts so that it seemed to bounce on the blue morning air. Then it disappeared into the trees.

"Bravo!" cried Sophie. And as I turned to look at her, heart pound-ing, alight with pride, my foot slipped.

If I hadn't fallen that October morning, would everything still have happened as it did?

"Dreams are the soul's sneezes."

My mother's voice. Opening my eyes, I found myself in bed, in my own room. There seemed to be two of her, and I waited, blinking, until they overlapped.

"You were dreaming," Mama said. "You were twitching and jerk-ing like a dog that dreams of rabbits."

Not rabbits. Legs, striped, ascending into a froth of petticoats—the innermost of which was the color of the hearts of roses—burned in my brain. When Mama's eyes met mine, I felt my face grow hot. She laid her palm across my forehead, my cheek. "Fever?" she murmured to herself.

"Mama—don't." I shifted away from her hand, and fire shot through my chest. A blurred kaleidoscope of images—wings, iron bars, blue-fire sky—whirled in my brain.

"You fell. Do you remember? In the orangerie. Sophie said you were after a bird. You broke two ribs on your left side. Does it hurt a lot?"

I nodded. When I breathed in, it felt as if I were being squeezed in a giant's fist.

Mama smoothed my hair back from my forehead. This time, I didn't move away. "Sleep, Charlie. Doctor Becker will be back this evening. He didn't want to wake you. Sleep, now."

Papa was in Quebec City on business. But Doctor Becker came (warm hands, cold stethoscope, fat gold watch on a gold chain), and my mother came (again and again, as is the nature of mothers), and Effie came (bouillon, buttered toast, a dose of Beecham's, chamber pot). Sophie came. My bedside lamp—turned low by Effie out of reverence for my condition—shed a glow of gaslight over her abundant flesh and made the whites of her eyes shine like boiled eggs. Altogether, I got as much attention as a thirteen-year-old boy could stand; no one reproached me for climbing the scaffolding, because my father thought boys should take risks. A boy who never injured himself never tested himself. *C'est ça.*

On the third morning Papa came. I woke to see him hesitating in the doorway. When he'd made sure I wasn't asleep, he came in and stood beside my bed. His mustache was gone. Dawn light seeping through the drawn curtains showed his upper lip, which (I realized with surprise) I had never before seen. Full as a woman's and as pink, it met his lower lip in a way that suggested, even to my innocent eye, desire and determination inextricably mingled. On some level far below words, I understood why he'd kept it covered. But why reveal it now?

The dawn dimness was noisy with waking birds (my mother believed all sickrooms should have open windows), and though I could see Papa's lips move, I couldn't hear what he said. I struggled to sit up. It hurt like the devil.

"You're better," he said. "*Grace à Dieu!*" When he smiled, his face looked less like a stranger's.

The bandages gripped my chest. Pain made me dizzy, but I nodded.

"You're better. But when will you be good?" His joke, perennial; his fiction, which I pretended to share, that I was brash and unpredictable, a taker of risks, a rebel.

He leaned toward me, and I thought for a moment he was going to embrace me, though that wasn't his way. Instead, he reached around me and extracted my pillow and pummeled it, then tucked it behind my head. The cool smell of starch from the pillowslip made me feel small again, and cared for.

Papa sat down at the foot of the bed, the way he used to do when I was seven, eight, nine years old. I'd wake in the twilight just before dawn to see his dim shape outlined in lifting darkness. "Oh—since you're up," he'd say. And he'd speak, in a quiet voice, about whatever was on his mind. His right-hand man at the factory drinking again; whether to hire an engineer, like the larger firms; the merits of a new kind of hemp from the Philippines. Less often, he'd talk about my mother. "Your mother" was how Papa referred to her, *ta maman*, as if investing me with some unique insight into the mysterious woman who was his wife. In those early morning conversations—or rather, soliloquies—he never asked me for advice, and of course I never offered any; yet I could feel, when at the edge of dawn he left, that he was somehow lighter.

Now I waited, as I always had. Now, instead of merely feeling his form at the foot of the bed, I could see it clearly, yet I had the sense of knowing less, rather than more, about his state of mind. There was only a feeling of tremendous energy held in check, a galvanized quality. A sort of readiness. Effie's voice sounded from the back stairwell, singing. *He took her by her lily-white hand, and kissed her mouth and chin. He led her to the water's edge and gently pushed her in.*

"Charles," my father said. *My father* was how I thought of him at that moment—not *Papa*—this mustacheless man whose eyes moved to the corners of the room and back. "There are things—how shall I put it?—things that one does because one wants to, and things that one does because one must. And, very rarely, things that are both. One day you will see. But even now, I know that you know this. Because of the bird."

He sat there at the foot of my bed for a long moment. The room was growing steadily lighter, but his eyes were in shadow. His hand grasped my ankle under the counterpane. A squeeze, a little shake, and then he left.

My mother was not so much mysterious as private. I didn't know her— no one knew her—but I never doubted her. If you *could* have entered her interior world, it would have made sense. She was all of a piece, as Effie used to say.

Convalescence. A crashing bore, Cordelia would have said. On the fourth day I was at last allowed out of bed, and, having mysteriously lost my taste for the novels locked behind glass in Papa's library, I decided to amuse myself by going through the trunks and barrels in the attic. This wasn't exactly forbidden, but it wasn't encouraged, either. I waited till late afternoon, when Effie was in the kitchen making butterscotch and singing (*Send me a kiss by wire. Baby, my heart's on fire.*), and Mama was out in the garden.

At the top of the attic stairs, the stored heat of the day lay in wait. It was like entering a dense cloud of butterflies. I pulled the stairs up after me, and the trapdoor clicked shut. The hot, still air smelled of mothballs and cedar. It made me feel odd, my head heavy and floating at the same time. Moving awkwardly—my ribs were still taped—I rummaged through some trunks of Mama's former finery, incomplete sets of china, old draperies brocaded with dust. At last I came to a little pearwood chest with mother-of-pearl inlay in the top. I thought it would be locked, but it wasn't. As I lifted the lid, its frayed silk lining gave way along one edge. Three small sepia photographs slid out.

The first showed a young woman in a pale suit cut in the reserved, graceful fashion of the 1890s. She'd begun to open a heavy carved wooden door but turned back to smile at the camera. Long hair coiled into a weight on her long neck. Wedding corsage of gardenias, lustrous as moonlight.

In the next photograph were two young women. Same heavy, shining hair; heads tilted at an equal angle, but only one of them beautiful. Hands behind their backs, they faced the camera with identical small, tucked-in smiles.

In the last photograph the bride stood between her cousin and a tall man with comb tracks in his hair and a clear, beautiful brow. The two women kissed each other on the lips, their faces obscured. The cousin and the groom held hands across the bride, who stood with her own hands thrust behind her, out of sight.

They weren't meant for me, or anyone, to see. Yet somehow I couldn't bring myself to return them to Mama's pearwood chest and close the lid. For some reason I thought of the retarded boy in my class at Holy Name—Mickey Dwyer, a legacy, accepted because his father and grandfather had gone there. His round face (already wearing the faint beginnings of a beard) was creased in a perennial expression of trying-to-think, and he worried each new event the way a dog worries a bone. He didn't know, but he knew that he didn't know. Like

Mickey—or rather, as I imagined Mickey—I felt as if there were a net
of considerations strung across the world, visible to others but invisible to me, and I kept walking into them. Kept entangling myself in
their sticky strands, like when I walked into a spiderweb spun, tight and
fresh, across the entrance to the Dugout.

When I went downstairs in the twilight before dinner, the house
was filled with sound. From the library off the foyer came the clack of
the new typewriting machine, which Sophie was learning to use. Slow,
a key at a time, an unsteady *tsk! tsk! tsk!* of disapproval. The door was
open. I could see a slice of candy-colored shirtwaist, a skein of dark-
gold hair thrown over one shoulder. In the room beyond, the room
that opened onto the unfinished orangerie, the workmen were finish-
ing up for the day. I could hear the rattle of bricks into a wheelbar-
row, the clang of metal on metal, a quick soft explosion of Portuguese.
From the kitchen came my mother's calm, clear voice interspersed
with Effie's deeper one.

Immaculate sounds. Sounds in their places; all as it should be.
And yet . . . My father whistled lightly between his teeth when he came
into the house that evening. "Be there in two shakes!" he answered,
when Effie stuck her head into the parlor to announce that dinner was
ready. *Two shakes.* That was Sophie's phrase. I'd never heard Papa use
it before she came. His voice sounded young—younger than I felt.

What I had seen and heard should have felt harmless, ordinary. It
didn't. It weighed on me. I wasn't even sure what secret I was keeping,
but I said nothing.

I have them still, the photographs I found that afternoon more than
half a century ago. I'm looking at them now, in the sunset light pouring in through my open window. Like me, they've faded. Below, on
Wickenden Street, I can see the young in one another's arms, flow-

ing hair and flowing garments, the summer sounds of Fox Point rising tinselly and joyful as a thousand banjos. The photos tremble slightly in my hands, and the late light illuminates every tortoise-like spot and wrinkle. I feel, God knows, my age and then some. And yet the realest part of me is still back there in the long golden autumn of 1911, fixed there by my silence as surely as these images are fixed in gelatin silver on this shivering paper.

Secrets keep us, not the other way around.

The sixth and last day of my convalescence—Doctor Becker had pronounced me fit to return to school, but Mama always liked a little margin—we spent in the garden, readying it for winter. After days of drawn curtains and liniment rubs and Effie's endless spoonfuls of cod liver oil, the garden seemed like heaven. Yet it held, despite the hot sunshine, an autumnal wistfulness. Mama must have felt it, too, because she murmured to herself, "'Seasons of mist and mellow fruitfulness, / Close bosom friend of the maturing sun.'" I trotted back and forth between the shed and the sundial with armloads of bedding straw while my mother collected rakes, trowels, twine, shears.

"'And they are gone: ay, ages long ago / These lovers fled away into the storm.' Take it easy, Charlie, please?"

I piled the bedding straw in the clearing around the sundial. It felt grand to be outdoors, to be moving, my chest now only lightly taped. Leaves floated down, bright as birds: scarlet from the maples, gold from the birches, yellow-green from the honey locusts. They lay in shining drifts across the flagstone paths that radiated out from the sundial, between the white and rust and yellow chrysanthemums, over the dry, flattened stalks of summer's irises and day lilies. All that glorious dying.

It was late morning. Friday, it must have been, because it was on a Sunday I freed the sparrow. My father had long since left for the factory; Sophie had gone on the streetcar to North Providence to see her dressmaker.

"Cousin Sophie's been here for almost three weeks," I said.

Mama handed me a rake. "We'll pile the leaves against the side of the shed, like we did last year. George can burn them when the weather's not so dry."

"Three weeks is a long visit."

My mother took the shears and began cutting back the roses that grew in a ring around the sundial. She had to crouch to do this, and she moved among the bushes without rising, on her haunches. She wore an old duster whose rusty black made her look like a huge crow, hopping and pecking. Here and there, a blowzy late bloom nodded on a yellowed stalk. *Snap!* went my mother's shears.

"Well?" I said. "Isn't it?"

"Sophie needs a rest. She's suffered trials."

For my mother the greatest source of life's trials was the male sex. Cousin Sophie's husband, then? No one had mentioned him since she'd arrived. I said, "Trials?"

I'd finished clearing one of the five flagstone paths. I piled the leaves at the end of it and leaned on my rake. The smell of the leaves was earthy and sharp in my nostrils. In some way it made me understand that I was no longer a child.

My mother had finished beheading the roses and was cutting lengths of twine. "Can't you rake any faster than that?" she said.

My father thought she ought to leave the yard to George, who after all was paid to take care of it. I knew Mama wanted to finish before Papa came home, as he generally did on Fridays, for lunch.

"What kind of trials?" I said.

The snap of the scissors slowed. Deliberately, I bore down through the leaves and dragged the metal tines of my rake across the flagstones. The sound was like the cry of a small wounded animal.

Mama leaned back on her heels and sighed. "Why does anyone hurt anyone? Why pick on somebody weaker than you? So you can comfort her afterwards, and in that way, comfort yourself?"

Raking assiduously, I kept my head down so my mother would not be reminded I was there. Mama's discussions with herself had always been one of my best sources of information.

"Maybe," she sighed. "Yes—perhaps. Masters beat their servants. Fathers take the strap to their children. Husbands strike their wives."

The husband. He and Sophie lived in Woonsocket, only an hour's ride on the Providence-Worcester Line, but they never visited us. I'd seen him only once, four or five years before. He came with Sophie to spend a Sunday afternoon playing croquet on the wide back lawn, and left abruptly, without explanation, before supper. But I remembered the small black eyes in the shadow of a seaman's brimmed cap, the square bear's body. Waldemar—that was his name.

"Or would you just lash out, to protect yourself? So as not to have to see that terrible fragility anymore? Not to have to know how fragile *you* are?"

And I remembered a story of rescue at sea, of many days on a life raft without food or water, Waldemar's companion having taken off his life vest and jumped out of the boat. I wasn't supposed to know about this—I'd been eavesdropping behind the dusty velvet folds of the parlor drapes. Because of its similarity to Papa's childhood experience, Waldemar's story had lodged in my mind and formed the stuff of nightmares. After I read about the Donner Party in one of Papa's books, cannibalism became part of them. What, my dreams demanded, had really happened to Waldemar's companion?

"Look!" cried my mother. By this time I'd finished raking the last of the flagstone paths. I shouldered my rake and went over to where she knelt among the yellowed stalks of gone-by flowers. Her hands cupped a small plant with heart-shaped, hairy leaves. Clearly a weed, I thought. Sheltered by hemlocks, it had hung on past summer. A few dry-looking clusters of flowers, deep reddish-purple, clung to its stem. My mother touched them with a fingertip.

"*Amaranthus retroflexus,*" she said. "I'd never have thought it would grow in this climate! Remember the seeds your uncle Thomas brought back from North Africa? Love-lies-bleeding, they call it there. Here it's called pigweed." She stroked the coarse leaves tenderly. "The Wife of Bath was fond of them. 'It tickleth me about my heart's root.' Of course, this one will die. But when I have my orangerie . . ."

She stood up, slapping her palms against her hips to dislodge the earth from them. Her face, upturned to the sky, shone with the snail tracks of tears. Surprised, I put my arm around her shoulders. She shook her head and moved away. Taking the other rake from where it leaned against the sundial, she turned and began to walk down the path to the gazebo.

"Spread that straw around the roses, would you?" she called over her shoulder. Duster billowing darkly around her, she disappeared into the shadowed recesses of the gazebo.

I knelt on the flagstones and began packing straw around the roots of the rosebushes. Now and then a thorn bit my fingers. Tears? My mother? It was so unlike her, such a breach of her privateness, that I was ashamed, as if I had come upon her naked. I breathed deep, inhaling the smell of earth and straw and decomposing vegetation, and I bent my thoughts to my work, as a man would do.

That smell. Years later, in the trenches of Belleau Wood, it would come to me, clear and pungent under the stench of urine and rotting flesh, and I would remember that October morning.

. . . .

The city streets wore Cordelia like a brilliant brooch when, on the following day, we went downcity together, as we'd done so often before. At first it was the same as always. The clang of the streetcar bell, the competing smells of electricity and horse dung, three boys at the back of the car, still in short pants, scuffling and whacking each other with their caps. Cordelia sat next to the window in a grass-green coat that followed her body closely, nipping in at the waist, and a grass-green skirt with a slit in front that showed her ankles. For the first time I understood how covering the body could make it more insistent, not less. Cordelia knew it, too. I could tell by the way she sat beside me, ankles crossing and uncrossing in shiny buttoned boots, hands uncharacteristically still in her grass-green lap. She smelled like carnations, faintly funereal.

Running down our street at noon, late for our meeting in front of Grace Church, I had planned to tell Cordelia everything. The photographs, my father's lost mustache, Sophie's ever-lengthening visit, my mother's distress. I thought if I talked to her it might all make sense. Cordelia would show me that my fears were groundless, that Papa's interest in Sophie was merely cousinly, that Mama was just going through one of her strange times. Now I hesitated. Cordelia's ankles, her perfume, made it impossible. I felt awkward beside her, callow, as young as the bare-kneed boys now shoving each other onto the floor behind us.

Cordelia muttered, "Oh, bugger!"

"What?"

"I forgot Mama's list. Bugger, bugger, *bugger!*" Cordelia snatched at her pockets, clicked her little beaded bag open and shut.

I said, "The butcher . . . the baker . . ."

Cordelia frowned, blowing upwards to lift the fringe of coppery hair off her forehead. Sweat shone on her upper lip. The afternoon was too warm for grass-green wool.

". . . the candlestick maker . . ."

She shot me a look meant to wither, then laughed instead.

At Market House the conductor went out of his way to hand Cordelia down the steps. The trolley tracks glittered like mercury in the hot sun. Cordelia's new boots skidded on them, and she would have fallen if I hadn't grabbed her arm. Her body pressed into my side for an instant, and my hand on her waist encountered the boniness of stays. A corset? Cordelia?

On the river a barge sounded its horn. We walked around to the back of Market House and watched the men unloading wooden crates of pineapples and bananas and oranges. The river breeze carried the smell of the ocean. Above our heads, seagulls skated on its updraft. They made a sound like angry babies, and the dockhands called to each other in Portuguese, and someone somewhere played a mournful tune on a harmonica.

In Goettner's Bakery the line of people waiting stretched through the open door and onto the pavement. We took our places at the end. Just ahead of us a nursemaid in a frilled cap and apron pushed a baby carriage the size of a small surrey. Cordelia made faces at the baby inside, swaddled in blankets and pink as an Easter ham from the heat. Time was, the faces she made would have been threatening—the two of us had always been sworn enemies of babies—but not now. Now there were sweet smiles and cajoling squeaks. How could I speak to this new cooing, corseted Cordelia about my fears?

A boy in knickers and an old, crushed fedora passed along the line hawking the *Daily Journal*. Two women behind us shooed him away, and he went off down the street shouting, "Yankees Drop Two Games to Sox! Foreign Warships Menace Newport! Only a nickel!" At the corner I saw him jump over a steaming coil of horse dung.

Cordelia pulled at her hair, fastened at the back of her head with a green-and-white-striped ribbon, and shook it out behind her. "If only I could put my hair up! I've asked and asked. But Mama is so very behind the times."

The nursemaid began struggling to push, then pull, the baby carriage up the two brick steps into the bakery. I stepped in front of Cordelia and lifted the front of the carriage. The nursemaid backed through the doorway. Between us we got the carriage inside. The line had shortened enough so that Cordelia and I could enter, too. Heat from the huge iron ovens at the back filled the small shop with the fragrance of baking bread.

"You *are* nice, Charlie," Cordelia murmured in my ear. Her breath felt like feathers. I studied the loaves of dark rye lined up on the counter, the rack of long serrated knives, Mrs. Goettner and her daughters bustling back and forth, but what I felt was Cordelia's body, the slope of her breasts, the curve of her waist. The clear print of a hand outlined in flour on the counter seemed like my thoughts made visible.

"If only Mama would let me put it up!" Cordelia was flapping her hair again: it was even hotter inside the bakery than it had been outside on the street. "Then I could wear hats. I'd wear really smart, distinctive ones, with ostrich plumes and pleated organdy. Hats like that one!"

Her arm grazed my chest as she lifted it to point. If only *I* had worn a hat! As it was, I had nothing I could use for concealment. I put both hands in my trouser pockets to even out the bulge and hunched my shoulders so that my jacket would go lower. Cordelia was still pointing out the window of the bakery. I turned to look.

Down the street, in front of the greengrocer's, a couple stood arm in arm looking up at something. The way they stood, their bodies touching, fitting into each other like two pieces in a puzzle, made me feel strange. Excited and afraid at once, so that I had to catch my breath.

The woman, whose broad back was turned to me, had one hand on the wide platter of flowers on her head. The man . . .

A carriage pulled up and obscured my line of vision. The driver got out to check the shoes on one of the horses. He took off his bowler and fanned himself with it. Then he walked around the carriage, checking the wheels. When he got back in and ambled off, the couple were still standing there, still locked together, looking now at each other. The woman, head tilted back, laughing, was Sophie. The man was my father.

I didn't tell my mother what I'd seen, or confront my father. If I had, would he have stayed with us?

Oh, one could just keep going back and back. Where does Papa's story start, really? Where does mine? My mother, as a little girl, sat on the lap of William James in her parents' house in Boston, twisting one of his lapels in her small hands.

What holds the world up? she asked him.

The world, he told her with the whimsy childless adults inflict on children, rests on the back of a giant turtle.

And what holds the turtle up? my mother persisted.

It rests on the back of an even larger turtle.

And that turtle?

James held up one large, freckled hand. It's no use, he said, and smiled. It's turtles all the way down.

In the parlor after dinner, my father and Sophie sat together on the slippery little Victorian sofa, passing the stereopticon back and forth. "Oh!" Sophie, every now and then, would say, so softly the word was no more than an indrawn breath. She gripped the binoculars in her fat hands and peered, entranced. Then she passed them to my father. Did

Papa's fingers stay for a second on hers? He lifted the stereopticon to his eyes and adjusted the focus.

"Charles!" he said, after a few moments. "Come and see this. You'd swear the creature was galloping straight toward you."

Reluctantly I left the jigsaw puzzle Mama and I were working—a picture of the battlefield at Gettysburg—and went over to the sofa. Papa handed me the heavy steel binoculars. They felt cold against my face. I squinted through them at a mild-looking brontosaurus pursued by two triceratops. There were some little brittle trees in the background, and a swooning lavender sunset. I could smell Sophie's scent, like grass in summer; she was so close that the warmth from her body radiated out to mine. Her skirt rustled faintly, like wind in the grass.

A log snapped on the fire. I pulled away. On the other side of the hearth Mama looked up from the puzzle and smiled. It was as if her heart traveled across the room to the three of us on an invisible pulley line, like the one on which Effie sent clean wet laundry out into the side yard on a sunny day.

Will Build to Suit ✥

KATHERINE LOOKED AROUND AT HER COMPANIONS—AS ALWAYS, there were two lines, the one you were in, and the one that moved faster—anxious, weary (the clock behind the counter said 05:26), and wearing the hangdog look of the luggageless. Businessmen in too-new jeans and costly running shoes, couples loudly taking each other for granted, one or two single women like herself. No children.

The sparkling sound of Italian reached her from the counter up ahead. She reminded herself that the airlines *always* lost her luggage. How many times in, what was it now, thirty-two years? But on those other trips—mostly to Eastern Europe, for digs or museum research or conferences—she'd stood in line with Theo. Had yawned, ridiculed, complained, cried (once), with Theo.

Nineteen hours now since she'd closed the door behind her in Providence, and already this trip had been the worst in her experience. Five days past September 11th, Logan had felt like an airport behind the Iron Curtain. Traveling citizens were corralled into a line that wound tightly back and forth under the gaze of booted guards and German shepherds. Spotlights beamed down on the long shining snouts of the guards' guns, on what seemed like miles of yellow tape holding everyone in place. Beyond the lights, the rest of Terminal E surrounded them, a moat of darkness. Looking up when her passport was demanded at last, Katherine half-expected to see a portrait of Lenin on the wall behind the stern Sabena ticket agent. And then the change of planes in Brussels, more lines, the makeshift curtained booth, the body search, confiscation of the nail file she'd carried in her purse since 1989. "Are you doing this with all passengers now?" Katherine had asked. "No," the uniformed woman had replied in her unpretty Belgian accent, "only those of America."

Now, at last, Rome. Even inside the airport she could smell it, the fragrance of Italy—like nowhere else in the world, Theo used to say. If they put me down blindfolded, he'd say, I'd know I was there.

"Sabena!" muttered a male voice behind her. "Stands for Such A Bad Experience—Never Again."

In spite of her exhaustion, she laughed. Turning, she saw first the beard—full, curly, graying—then the bearer of it. Tall and a little heavy, barrel belly under a patterned sweater, bruised-looking leather bomber jacket. He wore rimless glasses, behind which his eyes crinkled with humor. There was something about him Katherine found instantly likeable.

"You were on the flight from Boston," he said. His smile was likeable, too. She caught an undertow of Irish in his voice.

"Yes," she said.

She didn't *want* to like him. Didn't want to strike up a five a.m. acquaintance with someone she'd never see again. My life is full, she told herself. My heart is already hostage to more people than I can bear to lose. But he offered to get her a cappuccino if she'd hold his place in line. (Another flash of Poland twenty years ago, people asking, "Will you be standing?" when they wanted you to save their place while they went to wait in some other line.) When he brought back two paper cups in the colors of the flag of Italy, she drank gratefully, the bitterness of the cinnamon burning her tongue. Theo had always brought her coffee in the morning. It was his pleasure to make her feel cared for.

Slowly the line moved forward. They moved with it, a pair now. The man drank with clipped little sips, a sound not quite a slurp, the same sound her grandsons made. Katherine was aware of something in his stance—a spark. Interest. When he looked at her over the rim of his cup, his eyes crinkled likeably at the corners. She felt an answering spark somewhere inside—faint, but there. The first time since Theo died. Dismayed, she stepped slightly ahead, to reestablish the distance between them.

"What brings you to Rome?" he asked.

"I'm an archaeologist." She waited for the flicker of surprise. Instead, he said with interest, "Roman ruins, would it be, then?"

"Proto-Slavic," she said. "Inscriptions, mostly. Cyrillic. Glagolitic. I'm a paleographic archaeologist." Let him digest *that*, she thought.

"I build airports."

In her exhausted state this struck Katherine as funny. For the second time, she laughed. The man stood still. Offended? A shaft of sunrise reached them from the skylight; his rimless glasses became ovals of shine. He turned away. Impulsively, she reached out to put a hand on his arm, to say, *Wait—I didn't mean—* but as her fingers grazed the cool, scuffed leather of his jacket, a voice shouted, "*Signora! Prego, signora! A Le!*" She saw that it was her turn and moved up to the counter. A sleek young man offered the usual laminated card with photographs of two dozen different suitcases, none of which quite matched hers. When she'd finally, resignedly, selected its cousin and given her name and the address and phone number of the Society of American Scholars, she turned around. The builder of airports had disappeared.

Yes—a spark.

You're *allowed*, Debbie had said (Fourth of July night, bright-spangled sky, families reclining on their blankets), God, it's almost a year now, *Daddy* would've.

• • • •

They put her in the Greenhouse Apartment, the second story of a villa built by a long-dead pope for his mistress. A garden, pines, jewel-green grass. Keys the size of pocket wrenches unlocked a gate in the surrounding wall, then the carved double doors to the apartment itself. Katherine practiced until Anna Maria, the motherly woman in charge of visiting fellows, was satisfied. It would be dark, walking up the hill from the main building after dinner; the *signora professoressa* must be sure which key fit which lock, and how many turns each required.

Inside, her first impression was of gloom. Anna Maria moved along the far wall, pulling back curtains, opening windows. Sunlight (by now it was almost noon), pastel stucco, palm trees like flirting bright-green fans, a steep narrow street filled with children's voices and the stuttering of *motociclette*. She followed Anna Maria, who emitted a heady aroma of tobacco as she moved. Kitchenette, living room, small study overlooking the street, bedroom with a big brocade-covered bed.

Too much space for one person. Too much *bed* for one person.

"You will have now a little sleep," Anna Maria said. "I will telephone the airport concerning your luggage. Dinner will occur in the loggia, *apperitivi* at seven."

This apartment, Katherine knew from poring over the Society's brochure with Theo, was reserved for the most illustrious fellow in any given group. (*Distinguished guests are housed in the Villa Francesca, a fully appointed, self-contained accommodation half a block from the Society's main building.*) It was to honor Theo that they'd offered his fellowship to Katherine (whose reputation in the same field was so much less illustrious); it was to honor Theo that she'd accepted. She reminded herself of these facts as Anna Maria left, the screen door to the garden banging lightly behind her.

• • • •

The loneliness. Unprepared for it, despite Theo's long decline, she'd wandered around the house for weeks after he died, unscrewing grab bars, overseeing the removal of the stairlift, dismantling the remains of a life she'd thought insupportable and now would have given anything to have back. Even someone dying was someone to live for. *Especially someone dying.*

The part of Katherine that had moved out and up during Theo's dying—the part that seemed to regard her from a little distance, from a corner of the ceiling of his room—continued to hover and witness. *It's all right. Go ahead and cry. I'm here,* Ceiling-Katherine said to Katherine as she moved dimly through those first weeks. Gradually the voice changed from sympathetic to bracing. *You can do this. You'll survive—on your own.*

When she woke, the sun was setting. Katherine splashed cold water on her face, did what she could with her hair, straightened the clothes she'd been wearing for the last day and a half. Twenty-four hours now since Debbie and the boys had left her at the bus station. Debbie, having failed to talk her mother out of taking the trip at all, had refused to drive her to Logan ("Too dangerous, Mom. What if something more happens?"), and Timmy announced that he needed to throw up, and so there'd been no farewell to speak of. Suitcases on the sidewalk, a quick chorus of goodbyes.

Peering into the dim little bathroom mirror, she licked her index fingers and smoothed her eyebrows. She looked awful. If only she'd had the sense to bring a carry-on with toiletries and night things. But Theo had always been the one to do that. Theo, who loved travel for the same reason Katherine found it hard. When you're on the move, he used to say, anything can happen. Coincidence can find you.

The tolling of church bells through the open window mingled

with the noise of *motociclette* from the street below. Katherine rummaged in her purse for a lipstick and ran it carefully over her lips. This departure was to be the first of many. The start of the new Katherine. Unmoored: no one to arrive to, no one to leave. Here was the freedom she'd longed for, nights by Theo's hospital bed, breathing quietly, quietly, the better to hear him drown.

"—so finally the bartender says, 'You think I asked for a ten-inch *pianist?*'"

Laughter rose into the dusk. Waiters lit candles in the center of the two long tables, poured garnet-colored wine into goblets, set down silver trays of antipasti. (*Fellows are expected to gather each weekday evening for dinner, served until the beginning of November in the pleasant interior courtyard of the Society's main building.*) The woman sitting next to her shook back hair the length and color of Katherine's and gave her a look that was complicit, unamused: *Men.*

"Laura Sweeney from New Hampshire I'm a poet," she said, all in one breath, when Katherine introduced herself. She looked like the actress Cate Blanchett, fair, thin, her beauty spoiled—or saved?—by an unfortunate nose-to-chin ratio. Young, maybe early thirties. She could be me, Katherine thought, twenty years ago.

Across the table Laura's husband leaned back, shyly expansive, a man whose wife no longer laughed at his jokes. Matt Something—Carmody? Carmichael? By one of Theo's beloved coincidences, Katherine knew him. They'd met three years ago when he'd come to give a reading at Brown. He was kind. She remembered none of his poetry, but she remembered that. At the reception after the reading, Theo had tottered and nearly fallen and this Matt Whoever-He-Was had caught him—not just caught him but caught him discreetly, so that no one noticed. "Good save!" Theo had murmured. He'd still had his sense of humor then.

Up and down the long, damask-covered table, faces were dignified by candlelight. Conversation unfurled like music; clothes (*Fellows are expected to dress for dinner, men in jackets and ties, women in skirts, either long or street-length*) were stately. Katherine pulled down the sleeves of her white cotton pullover and drained her wineglass. Spaghetti with mushrooms and gorgonzola, some kind of plump white fish, a sharp-tasting green salad, each course accompanied by its own wine. There were more people at the table (covertly, she counted) than Katherine had expected. Nineteen *distinguished scholars, writers, and artists from every part of the United States*, give or take a few spouses. Theo's reputation had preceded him here, as it did everywhere they went together. (Her own—well, she'd done respectable work in her field, but work had always come second to life. Her life with Theo.) She heard a white-haired woman at the head of the table say Theo's name to the man beside her. The man to Katherine's right (composer, Nebraska) wanted to know whether any musical instruments had been discovered in Theo's dig in the Ukraine.

Full dark, now. An occasional lull in the conversation admitted, from the courtyard, the warnings of cicadas. Katherine's own research (which no one except Laura Sweeney asked about) involved inscriptions carved into resistant materials. She told Laura how, on the tombstones of Englishwomen whose husbands had died before them, in the sixteenth and seventeenth centuries, they put, not *Wife* of So-and-So, not *Widow*, but *Relict. Here lies Abigail Chase, Relict of Samuel.* From the Latin, meaning "remainder, something left behind." Laura snorted at that, as Katherine had known she would.

A little girl left the children's table to come and stand between her mother and Katherine, twisting one leg around the other. "Hi," Katherine said. The child looked up at her from under fine blonde eyebrows. "What's your name?"

"Amber Sweeney-Carmichael. I'm five."

"Hey!" Matt Carmichael said to Katherine from across the table, interrupting the monologue of a ferret-like woman (semiotics, San Diego) in a red satin jacket. "I remember you." (And why not? Katherine thought. It wasn't every day that someone's two-hundred-and-twenty-pound husband fell on you. Or maybe his own heroism had embedded the incident in his mind.) They talked about his visit to Providence, about places there that had found their way into the poems in his new book. By the time dessert appeared, followed by brandy in fragile crystal globes, this slim connection had turned into one of those quickly forged bonds that the prospect of a year among strangers—bright, argumentative, competitive strangers—always seemed to evoke.

Making her way back uphill through the fragrant darkness to the Villa Francesca, Katherine felt less like a refugee. She was warmed through from the wine and the brandy. Laura had lent her a woolen sweater and a nightgown, and pressed on her one of the books she and Matt had shipped from the States, the collected poems of E. E. Cummings. A thin, bespectacled man (Slavicist, North Carolina) had offered to walk her back to the pope's mistress's villa, but she'd declined. A little sociability, a little kindness—that was all she'd needed. Nothing more than that; no one closer than that. Under her arm she carried, besides the book and the ring of heavy keys, Amber's second-best stuffed animal, a green velvet elephant with impossibly large ears.

Bed was the place where they gave and received pleasure, even asleep, even angry, their bodies touching in sleep like puppies. Littermates, Theo called it.

Waking, she was so sure the phone had rung that she grabbed for it in the dark, knocking the alarm clock off the bedside table. But when she held the receiver to her ear, there was no one.

How many times, all last autumn, had this happened? The certainty that the phone had woken her—its clear, peremptory echo in her ear—then only the dial tone and, when she called the skilled desk, the assurance of the night nurse that, no, nothing had happened, Theo was safe and sound. (Report from Planet Morphia, Katherine's son-in-law called this.) So many times, that finally Doctor Gazzerro had sent her to a neuropsychiatrist, a brisk Israeli woman a decade younger than Katherine who explained, with diagrams, about auditory hallucinations and stress. Reptiles, having no limbic brain and therefore no emotions, had no hallucinations, she said. (How on earth did researchers determine that?)

Now, high up in a corner, Ceiling-Katherine spoke. *You're okay! You're on your own, but you're fine.*

Sitting up in bed under all the blankets the pope's mistress's villa had to offer, Katherine pulled Laura's sweater more closely around her. In autumn the Roman night entered your bones, Anna Maria had warned the Fellows at dinner, colder than the sunny days allowed one to imagine, and Italian law forbade the use of central heating until November. Shivering, Katherine switched on the thoughtfully placed bedside lamp (*Fellows will be expected to read in bed on a nightly basis?*) and reached for Matt's book.

> sometimes i am alive because with
> me her alert treelike body sleeps
> which I will feel slowly sharpening
> becoming distinct with love

Katherine turned out the light and settled into the pillows with Amber's velvet elephant tucked in the crook of her arm. Oh, E. E.! she thought, e(ternally) e(nergetic), what an optimist you were. As if paradox explained anything. What help is it, to get the contradiction right? Roman days, no matter how luminous and warm, are followed by Roman nights.

He loved her midriff. That was the word he used, *midriff*. He liked her to lie on top of the bedspread with her hair spread out around her head like (he said) gold wire and her back arched so that he could trace her ribs with his warm fingers.

In the morning she slept late, woke up in a state her son-in-law would have called sleep-depraved, longing for coffee. There was nothing in the little kitchenette except a few packets of sugar stolen from a nearby *trattoria*. She splashed water on her face, put on the same dank jeans and airport-smelling cotton pullover she'd spent the last two days in, and took her headache out into the sunshine. This morning the keys gave her an argument. She had a moment of steeply ascending panic: as terrifying to be locked in as to be locked out. Then the door yielded, and she was out on the street, narrowly missed by a *motocicletta* whose unhelmeted rider turned around to shout, "*Salami!*"

They were sitting in green-painted lawn chairs under the ancient pines with books in their laps. Matt and Laura. The chairs were placed at a slight angle to each other, and they held hands across the broad wooden arms as they read, their apartness at dinner the night before having been mended (Katherine could feel it) by sex. Amber sat nearby with a couple of stuffed animals. The shadows of the pines lay like liquid on the grass. Katherine, the sudden itch of tears under her lids, crossed the lawn to walk unnoticed under the portico. Safe in the little bar, she ordered in uncertain Italian, remembering too late that espresso was for late day, cappuccino for morning. The place was empty except for two men who looked as if they worked on the grounds, speaking a

rapid sewing-machine Italian Katherine couldn't imagine ever crack-
ing. Probably all the other Fellows had dispersed to the city's libraries
(*Autoritazioni will be provided for facilities required by Fellows in the
pursuit of their Research*), where they sat surrounded by leather-bound
volumes smelling of mice. Would *she* ever work, really work, again?
Would it matter to anyone if she did?

She opened the book Matt had lent her and read the first thing her
eyes fell on.

> your homecoming will be my homecoming—
> my selves go with you, only I remain;
> a shadow phantom effigy or seeming

She closed the book and sat looking out at the blue-shadowed courtyard. The fountain in the center made a quiet unceasing sound, water
into water.

Homecoming, she thought. And for no reason at all the image of
the Builder of Airports flashed across her mind, with his likeable eyes,
his likeable smile. She felt the itch of tears again. It's only the poem,
she told herself. The sight of Matt and Laura on the lawn. But it was as
if a tiny crack in her heart—a hairline fissure she hadn't even known
was there—had widened, just a little. They could have been her and
Theo, the couple she'd just seen, two chairs, heads bent, hands touching in the dappled light. Her and Theo in Warsaw in 1980, in that
warm, wine-y autumn, the autumn of Solidarity and strikes and Lech
Walesa. Were they the ghosts, or was she? Had she wandered for a
moment into her own past, lost or intruding, not real at all, despite the
warmth of Laura's sweater around her shoulders?

Go for a walk, Ceiling-Katherine advised from a high corner
between two stone cherubs. *Get out and about.* Katherine drained her

cup and sucked the pulp from the slice of lemon. Its sourness made her shiver. She pushed back her chair and went out, through the court-yard, through the iron gates, to the Via Angelo Masina. *Many interesting parts of Rome lie just across the river from the Society. Fellows will particularly enjoy the Roman Forum, the gardens of the Villa Borghese, the Capuchin Capel built out of human bones.* Instead, on impulse, Katherine began to walk down the hill. Perverse of her, on her first day in the Eternal City, not to visit some of its more famous sights—not only perverse but capricious, the one thing a caregiver could not ever be. The morning air was still and sweet.

That night, not up to the luxury, the candlelight, the inquiries of her fellow Fellows, Katherine skipped dinner. *Jet lag, that's all*, was Ceiling-Katherine's diagnosis. She bought a mozzarella-and-tomato sandwich at the little bar and took it, along with a Campari-soda, back to the Greenhouse Apartment. The TV at the foot of the bed offered only a quiz program or the news. Katherine couldn't make out a word except *arrivederci*. She got up and put her dishes in the sink and took off her clothes—the pants and sweater that were by now far too famil-iar, the underwear that, once again, she washed and hung over the shower bar—and got into bed with Matt's book.

> my love is building a building
> around you, a frail slippery
> house, a strong fragile house

That night, it wasn't the phone that woke her, but a dream. The Builder of Airports appeared at the foot of the bed. He came closer. He handed her his card. There was a symbol on it she recognized as Glagolitic, and beneath it the words, "Will Build to Suit."

Waking, she was surprised to feel sadness. She thought, I don't even know his name.

"I meant what I said, and I said what I meant. / An elephant's faithful, one hundred percent," Katherine recited to Amber. She held out the green velvet elephant. "Thank you for lending me this."

Amber reached out to finger the edge of Katherine's sweater. Her third day in Rome, and Sabena was still pursuing her luggage, last seen in Milan.

"That's my mom's," Amber said, "it's her *favorite*," then turned and ran, through alternating sun and shadow, to where Laura stood at the far end of the loggia.

Katherine tucked the elephant under one arm and bent to pick up the jump rope that lay coiled serpentlike in the dewy grass. Rolling the wooden handles between her palms, she remembered Debbie at five, in her blue school uniform, her fair hair braided tightly and looped behind her ears (as she demanded, like her schoolmates'), her high voice fluting Polish jump-rope rhymes. Remembered "The Voice of America" on the radio at breakfast, with its magisterial, halting Special English: *Russian troops are massing on the Polish border.* Remembered the small suitcase under their bed, carefully packed by Theo—passports, American dollars, candy bars, cigarettes (neither of them smoked)—in case of evacuation. In case Russian tanks came trundling across the bridge over the Vistula into the Old City, where they lived.

"Thank God school starts tomorrow," Laura said when Katherine reached her. Despite the morning chill, she wore jeans and a yellow silk vest; between them gleamed several inches of smooth, tanned stomach. "I haven't written a word since we got here. Unlike Matt." Again that complicit look.

The space beneath the portico was filled with violet shadows. Amber stood with her arms clasped around her mother's hips. In one hand Laura held a book; the other hovered, not quite touching her daughter's yellow hair.

Katherine could almost feel its fine slipperiness. "I could take her," she said, impulsively. "For the afternoon. We could go for a walk. Would you like that, Amber?"

Laura hesitated. Amber turned her face to her mother's blue-jeaned hip. Did she nod, or was she just burrowing?

But it didn't matter which. Laura put her hand on Amber's head and tipped it back. Mother and child looked at each other. Katherine couldn't see Amber's face, but she saw Laura smile: dimples of iron.

Several rooks flew down and began to troll the flowers that bordered the loggia, releasing the impersonal odor of chrysanthemums into the still air. Katherine held out the jump rope and (with a tiny, surprising tug of reluctance) the velvet elephant, and Laura took them.

Laura made up her mind. "That would be *great*. After lunch? We'll meet you right here."

Amber clapped her hands in delight. The rooks, startled, rose up from the flower bed in a single motion. Their dark wings beat the air as they soared, cawing, up over the loggia roof.

Laura, Laura, Katherine thought, watching them fly away. Don't you know what you have?

Four years—he's been sick for four years, she'd said to her son-in-law shortly before Theo died. The two of them were sitting on the window-sill in the dark beside his hospital bed, very late at night, a half-full moon setting behind the three round blue smokestacks of the Narragansett Power Station. Katherine watched the jewel-like red lights on top of them blink on and off.

I've been taking care of him for four years. In four years I could've gone through college all over again.

You have, Dave said.

Afternoon light deepened everything, made colors saturated and intense, like colors from a child's paintbox. Amber's hand in Katherine's was warm and firm as they walked along the tree-lined street descending toward the Tiber, with its greengrocers and small shops, its pregnant women and bakeries and babies. Geraniums in pots lined the windowsills of narrow stone houses, bright as splashes of blood. Amber stopped still on the brick pavement and threw her head back. Katherine did the same. The sun through the leaves splashed her face with green-gold light, then shadow, and a bird, hidden from view, poured down a stream of song. Amber laughed out loud. Katherine did the same. *You see?* said Tree-Katherine. *You're fine.*

They followed the street down and down. The smells of Italy— flowering shrubs, brick dust, tobacco, baking bread—wrapped around them as they walked. Amber chattered. "Can you do the tango? I can. I can *try*." (Stepping over a dog turd in the middle of the pavement:) "That reeks!" (Watching a woman in a harlequin suit cross a small piazza on stilts:) "I wish I was invincible."

They reached a greengrocer's stand at the bottom of the hill. The white-aproned proprietor came around a table of pineapples and grapes and pomegranates, and said, "*Buongiorno, signora! Desidera?*" On his shoulder sat a small striped owl.

Amber's grip on Katherine's fingers tightened. Katherine could feel her quivering, though she stood quite still.

"Do not fear," the man said to Katherine. "She don't travel."

On Amber's small, upturned face was an expression of pure delight. "What's her name?" she asked the greengrocer. "How old is she?"

His face, plump but handsome, creased in answering delight. He shrugged. At the movement, the owl stiffened. It lifted one leg and flexed the talons slowly, showily, then sank them into the greengrocer's shoulder. The man said something to it in Italian. The owl's head turned, kept turning, swiveled all the way around. Amber laughed.

"*Bene!*" the greengrocer cried. He put a hand into his apron pocket and brought out something pinched between thumb and forefinger. Katherine saw it wriggle. He held it up to the owl, whose beak snapped, once, a small, decisive click. Its feathers swelled until it was nearly twice as wide. Its yellow eyes regarded them.

"Oh!" breathed Amber.

The man delved into his pocket again and held out a small, dark, wriggling thing. Amber reached for it.

"Amber Sweeney-Carmichael!"

Laura brushed past, pushing Katherine aside. She grabbed Amber's arm. Katherine couldn't see her face, but her voice was a clenched mother-voice. "What do you. Think you're. Doing?"

"*Buongiorno, signora! Desidera?*" The proprietor tucked the small wriggling thing back into his pocket and, as plump and gleaming as his produce, motioned to Laura to stroke the rough skin of an avocado.

"Well?" Laura demanded. A question meant, not for her daughter, but for Katherine. She turned on her a face red with righteousness. "I just had this feeling. I just suddenly *knew*: Amber's in danger."

Amber said, "Mama—look! It's a real owl!"

The greengrocer held a pineapple up to his nose and sniffed dramatically. He gestured toward grapes in three shining heaps, purple, green, and black. On his shoulder the owl flapped its wings and resettled itself.

Katherine said, "Laura. It's perfectly safe. She never even—"

"What do you want, hanging out with a five-year-old? Why don't you go and do your work?"

The greengrocer reached into his apron pocket—the other pocket, Katherine noted with relief—and produced a bright-red apple-shaped lollipop. Its stick was a twig holding two green paper leaves. Amber looked at it with longing.

But Laura had already begun to walk away, pulling Amber with her. "We don't take. Presents. From strangers."

The greengrocer smiled his incomprehension and held out the candy.

"Bye, Katherine," Amber said. Her voice sounded wistful but resigned. She was walking backwards, her eyes on the owl, her mother dragging her by the arm. Laura quickened her pace. They left the greengrocer standing there, still bewildered, still holding out his hand.

Katherine bought a paper cornet of clementines she knew she wouldn't eat, said, "*Grazie*" and (her scant Italian not up to more) "*Arrivederci*," and walked on, toward the river.

A piazza thronged with pigeons. A medieval cloister. A sun-filled square of orange trees and jasmine whose fragrance reached for her as she walked by. Laura was right, of course. She, Katherine, should be working again by now, inhabiting (or at least building) her own life, looking toward the future—not trying, through someone else's child, to resurrect the past. From somewhere ahead came the sound of an organ-grinder. The hurdy-gurdy melody beckoned and, as if she were a child, her heart lifted. She began walking toward it. The narrow street curved. Ahead was a sort of tunnel. No—an underpass, and at the end of it, a wedge of sunlight, a little knot of people. She walked under the low, massive arch. Its shadows held the exhalations of ancient stone, cindery and bitter, and then, suddenly, the smell of open urinals somewhere nearby.

Bringing Theo's clothes home from the hospital, that last time. When she untied the plastic bag the ER nurse had given her, the stench of urine nearly knocked her down. Holding her breath, pulling things out of the bag to put them in the washer, as if they would someday be worn again, she found everything—faded blue work shirt, khakis, undershirt, boxers printed with little black keys—in pieces. They'd had to cut the clothes off him.

Katherine stood still, in the dark center of the underpass. One hand went out to steady herself. The stones against her palm were cold and slick with moss. She pulled her hand away and ran.

The bridge rose in front of her, ancient blue-gray stone, offering the city on the other side of the river, green glints of cypress, golden domes. Katherine ran onto the narrow cobbled walkway, slowed, then stopped. People brushed past; she heard rapid Italian, laughter. Breathing hard, she leaned her arms on a ledge of warm stone. She was still clutching the clementines. She set them down where the ledge broadened, their paper wrapping soggy with sweat. On the bank of the river, poplars had turned a smoky gold and begun to let go of their leaves. She looked down. The Tiber was slow and laden with silt, yellow leaves falling into yellow water. Sun warmed the top of her head. It could have been a touch—Theo's touch. Theo's hand. *My selves go with you.*

But it wasn't; they didn't. With a shock of suddenness, like a chill gust off the river, she knew that. It was no longer Theo she mourned. It was who she had been, with him.

When had it happened, this change? How had she missed it? She did not want this new, changed grief. It cracked her heart open— cracked *her* open. She was unprotected. Anything could enter.

Of their own accord, Katherine's hands made a quick rejecting motion. The clementines fell with a distant splash into the Tiber.

Like a dreamer struggling to awake, Katherine forced herself to look around the table. Matt and Laura, sitting next to each other, elbows touching, looked back at her; Laura smiled forgivingly. In the candlelight a preacher-voiced man (international water rights, Texas) regaled the table with the latest news from the States. Katherine picked up a glass at random and drank. The sting of Campari in her throat assured her that she was real, corporeal, made of flesh that could still feel pleasure and pain. *Pay attention!* Ceiling-Katherine advised from a corner of the portico roof. *Stay in the present.* There'd been another plane crash, the water-rights activist said, they weren't sure yet what caused it. And a man, an Arab, on the Amtrak train from Boston to New York, had been caught carrying a knife and taken off the train at Providence—

A man at the foot of the table, professor *emeritus* of something-or-other at Columbia, interrupted to complain about being served prosciutto on Rosh Hashanah.

"Providence?" Katherine said, alarmed, but the conversation had moved on. "Providence?" she asked the woman next to her (psychiatrist, Chicago), who nodded. The candlelight gave her a wise, whiskery look, like a catfish.

In Warsaw that autumn, Theo had gone to the American Embassy to see the Press & Culture attaché. What do we do if the Russians invade? he demanded. What's the evacuation plan? Stay by your phone, the man said; we'll call and tell you what to do.

"Fucking idiots!" Theo paced the bedroom of the little apartment on Swiętokrzyśka Street at midnight, damping his fury so as not to wake Debbie. "If the Russians come, it'll be a race between them and the Poles to see who cuts the phone lines."

The very next day he met a man at the American Club bar, the chief of operations for Pan Am in Eastern Europe, who (another of Theo's beloved coincidences) had once worked as a pin-boy in Theo's uncle's bowling alley. If the Russians invade, come immediately to the airport, this man said. Bring one suitcase for the three of you. There'll be a plane waiting.

She woke in darkness to the telephone's urgent reverberations. Grabbing for it, she heard the alarm clock hit the floor, then silence. The phone wasn't ringing. The room's black stillness told her it hadn't *been* ringing.

She switched on the bedside lamp and, leaving the alarm clock on the floor where it had fallen, opened Matt's book. But the words on the page wavered, then blurred. She felt tears begin to crawl, one after another, down her cheeks. They fell onto the borrowed book, the borrowed sweater. This is ridiculous, she thought; he's been dead more than a year, it's been months since I . . . She tried to stop. Instead, without warning, she began to laugh—laugh *while* she cried—and she couldn't stop doing that, either. Sobs and cackling poured through the room, voluptuous and terrible. On the floor the alarm clock's glowing red numerals, upside-down, read, "hE:11."

Am I going crazy? she thought. Then: No. This was her new, changed grief. This was what it felt like, to be open.

She was cold—so cold. Her fingers seized the edges of Laura's sweater and held on. She waited for Ceiling-Katherine to speak. But the only sounds were her own.

The morning was blessedly gloomy. She called home as soon as she woke up. Her son-in-law's voice answered, gravelly and thick.

"We're fine, Kat. Do you know what time it is here?"

"Oh, God. I'm sorry—I didn't think." *A frail slippery house.*

"It's okay. Don't stress about it. Look, we're all fine, and we'll talk to you soon. Okay?"

"Brendan? Timmy?" *A strong fragile house.*

For the third time Dave assured her everyone was fine—the Arab on the Amtrak train had been about to peel an apple—then sang a chorus of "Waking Up Is Hard to Do." They said goodbye, and Katherine hung up.

Copper-colored rumors of sunrise were quickly swallowed up by clouds, and the dew on the grass, as Katherine crossed the courtyard, barely shone. She drank cappuccino in the little bar, alone at this early hour. When footsteps sounded under the portico, she rose and went in through the *salotto* and down the echoing stone corridor. Anna Maria's little office, filled with leaning stacks of books, smelled of freesias and stale tobacco.

"*Signora!*" Anna Maria, standing behind her desk with an armful of papers, looked up and smiled. "*Che buona fortuna!* Francesco has just now told me that your luggage arrives. He carries it to the Greenhouse Apartment. You will be happy to have your things, I am sure." Her glance traveled quickly over Katherine's pullover, which by now looked like somebody had sneezed into it, and stopped at Katherine's face. "But something goes wrong? You look to have quite problems."

No way to explain that the New Katherine she'd come to Rome in search of was not the one she'd found. Katherine said, "*Grazie.* Thank you for looking after the luggage. For everything. I'm sorry, but I'm afraid I must go home. The situation in America . . . you understand. If something more happens—"

I don't want to be on the other side of the ocean from my daughter and my grandsons and my son-in-law (who makes me laugh) and my husband's ashes.

Of course she didn't say this. And Anna Maria didn't point out that all the other Fellows were staying.

•   •   •   •

The road to the airport was a procession of pale lights glimmering in the deep-dish blue of the half hour before dawn. Katherine watched them pass, both arms wrapped around her rib cage as if to keep her new kind of grief from kibitzers. As if to re-enclose herself—though she knew it was already too late. Her cabdriver, unusual for an Italian *tassista*, was silent. This suited Katherine. She'd skipped dinner the night before—unable to face the compassion of Matt and Laura, the good-byes and good lucks of the other (the strong, the staying) Fellows—and now was skipping town.

The driver pulled up at an unmarked loading dock and, without speaking, carried her bags up an untrafficked flight of stairs and through a series of covered walkways to the sudden bright bustle of the terminal, where he accepted her generous tip and bowed and left her.

The line for the Sabena check-in desk wound unnecessarily back and forth between silver stanchions. Her fellow passengers could have been the same ones she'd come here with: the carping couples, the business travelers in ironed bluejeans, the single women of a certain age. Herding her luggage in front of her, Katherine shuffled along. The man in front of her said into his cell phone, "I'll call you Thursday, just to sync up. We'll dialogue." Her two bags, which she'd never even unpacked, should have seemed like mute testimony to Katherine's failure. She had not allowed this trip to unfold as she and Theo had planned, had not accepted the experience of his beloved Italy which he had, in a sense, bequeathed to her. Three days—that was how long the New Katherine had lasted. Yet she felt a sense of—not lightness, exactly—spaciousness. Like stepping out into the garden in her night-gown, first thing in the morning.

"They're killers, these quick trips. Don't you find?"

Faint Irish lilt. She turned—and there, improbably, he was.

"Do you not remember me, then?" Curly graying beard, bomber jacket, belly. His eyes crinkled, appealing.

Her heart tilted upward. "I remember," she said. "You build airports."

His smile broadened. "Gene O'Casey." He held out a hand.

Katherine hesitated. Her own hand was shaking. Then she grasped his. The palm was callused and cool, the fingers firm around her own.

"Katherine. Katherine Hagesfeld."

In his other hand was a paper cornet of glossy black grapes. He said, "Do you know what they call these, then? In the region where they come from?"

A large woman in a red kerchief tried to push past. The tide of waiting passengers shifted, bumping Katherine, who stumbled forward. She kicked her bags, and one fell over onto its side. Gene O'Casey's hand under her elbow steadied her. He held out the paper cornet of grapes. Smiling her thanks, she pulled one, then another, off their stem and put them into her mouth. The grapes burst on her tongue, sweet and slow. Gene O'Casey bent down and righted her suitcase.

"They still haven't found mine," he said.

About the Author ❈

Photo by Michael Rosen

ANN HARLEMAN is the author of *Happiness*, a story collection that won the Iowa Short Fiction Award, and the novel *Bitter Lake* (SMU, 1996). She's been the recipient of Guggenheim and Rockefeller fellowships, three Rhode Island State Arts Council fellowships, the Berlin Prize in Literature, the PEN Syndicated Fiction Award, an O. Henry Award, and a Rona Jaffe Writer's Award. In an earlier life, she was the first woman to receive a Ph.D. in linguistics from Princeton, and she lived and worked behind the Iron Curtain. Now she is on the faculties of Brown University and the Rhode Island School of Design, where she teaches fiction writing to visual artists.

Visit her Web site at www.annharleman.com.